Evalycer's War

I0459954

By

Margena Adams Holmes

Copyright 2019 by Margena Adams Holmes

This is a work of fiction. Names, places, characters, and events within this novel are from the author's imagination. Any resemblance to actual people, living or dead, or to any event is purely coincidental.

No part of this work may be reproduced, photocopied, transmitted, or otherwise used without the prior written consent of the author, except for brief excerpts for review purposes only.

Book cover by Ian Bristow. Thank you!

Thanks to Leslie E. Heath for being my honest beta reader.

I'd like to thank my family—Reid, Aerin, Brent, Carter, and Wolfe—for their love and support throughout this journey of writing and editing.

The bell rang, releasing students from classes for the day at Star-Bound Primary School, but a blonde-haired girl sat in a chair in the school office, arms folded across her chest. She watched through the window as her mother spoke with the principal of the school. While the principal appeared to be calm, hands clasped loosely in front, the girl's mother was anything but. Evalycer Nicholls could tell by her mother's squinty eyes and furrowed brow.

Her mother shook hands with the principal and hit the button to open the door.

"Come on," her mother commanded.

Evalycer immediately stood and followed her mother out of the office and the school. She knew better than to say anything until they got into the land-rover.

"You have got to watch what you say, Evalycer," her mother Miranda said quietly, inputting the code to start the vehicle. It began to hum as the engine engaged.

"I can't help if she can't handle the truth about what she wears," Evalycer said.

Her mother sighed. "Think before you speak, child. You have to respect people and their feelings. Calling someone a Caledonian fruit fly isn't constructive or nice."

Evalycer smiled to herself. The girl in question did look like a Caledonian fruit fly with her billowy red dress making her look like she'd sprouted wings on her body.

"Even if it's true?"

"Even if it's true."

An only child, Evalycer tried to get along with other kids, but they never seemed to like her much. She was smart and funny, but her lack of tact and her habit of saying whatever came into her head made other kids stay away from her. Her only friends were a brother and sister—twins—in her fifth year class. It didn't make them popular, either, being friends with Evalycer. As the daughter of one of the teachers at the school, Evalycer was held to a higher standard, so anything she did almost always got her into trouble.

Traffic was light at that time of day and her mother pulled up to their tan dome-shaped home a few minutes later.

"Go to your room until I tell you to come out," she told her daughter as she waved her keycard at the sensor. The door swung open.

"Yes, ma'am," Evalycer said.

Evalycer went to her room and shut the door. She'd rather be home in her room, anyway. It gave her time to study the galaxy. She wanted to be a pilot when she grew up. Even as a small child she'd always been fascinated by the stars and wanted to learn what she could about the universe. Now, at ten standard years old, she could read about all the planets in the Ennek System and beyond.

She turned on her computer at her desk and started reading about the different constellations, forgetting about the homework she should to be doing. She could read for hours about the planets and their systems.

Her father's voice in the other room brought her back down from the stars. She hurriedly turned off the computer and jumped onto her bed, picked up her tablet, and pulled up one of her school books she should be reading. There was a knock on her door.

"Come in," she said.

Her father Jaiy, a security guard for the governor of Ennek, stepped into her room. He stood tall over her small bed, looking down at his daughter.

"Mother tells me that you got in trouble again today," he said.

"Yes sir," Evalycer mumbled.

"Want to tell me what happened?"

4

Evalycer put her tablet down and told her father everything that happened.

"I wasn't trying to be mean, honest," Evalycer finished. "It just came out."

Her father sat down on the foot of her bed. "I know it's hard, but please try to be more kind," he said. "There's too much negativity in the universe without adding to it."

Evalycer looked at her father, who smiled.

"I promise to try to do better," she said.

"Good girl," he said, standing again. "Now, what planet system have you been reading about today?"

Evalycer's eyes widened in surprise. "How did you…"

"I know you, Lyci. You'd rather read about the stars than do your math homework."

Her father smiled and playfully pulled on a strand of hair before going out to change out of his uniform and get ready for dinner.

After dinner, Evalycer started on her homework and finished before bedtime. When she came out of her room to tell her parents good night, her father called her to the back balcony of their home. He had set up his high-powered starscope and had it aimed at her latest planet system obsession.

"If you look through here," he said gently, "You can see the Ornocto System."

Evalycer stood on her tiptoes to look through the scope. She could see the bright yellow sun of the Ornocto System with its five green-blue planets around it, each planet progressively darker the further away it orbited from the sun.

"They are the only system in our part of the universe that has a mono sol system, so all the planets in that system revolve around the same sun," her father told her. "The rest of the planets in this region have their own smaller suns that they orbit around."

"Ornocto's system is more like Earth's system?" Evalycer asked, referring to her previous obsession in the universe.

"Yes."

Evalycer stepped away from the scope and her father looked into it again, moved it slightly to the right and adjusted the focus on it. He backed away to let Evalycer look through it again.

"That's Startia, in the Darantha System," he told her.

The tiny far-away planet shone blue and yellow in the sun it revolved around.

"What's that brown stuff to the left?" she asked.

"That's the asteroid field that separates Startia and Foridian. You have to be escorted by security to get through it safely."

Evalycer looked in awe at the planet system so far away. She hoped to be able to visit there and other places someday.

"I see you going to many different places in your life," her father said. "But you have to get through school first, and that means not getting in trouble."

"I understand," she said. "I'll do better."

"Good girl," he said, giving Evalycer a hug as she turned to look through the scope again. "Now, I know you can never get tired of looking at the stars, but if you don't want to fall asleep in class tomorrow, you'd better scoot off to bed."

"Aw, already?" Evalycer said, slumping her shoulders.

"Yes."

Evalycer kissed her father's cheek and ran off to her room.

Chapter Two—The Move

Evalycer tapped her fingers on the armrest of the chair as she bounced her right leg, trying to figure out why her mother had been called into a meeting.

I know I didn't do anything wrong...today.

Had she known this meeting would take so long, Evalycer could have gone to hang out with her friends at the park next to the school to check out the boys there. At thirteen years old, she found boys...interesting. Most boys, though, weren't interested in looking at the stars at night. They just wanted to play video games, which was fun and all, but Evalycer would rather be outside.

The sound of the office door sliding open brought Evalycer out of her thoughts. Her mother came out from the office with a smile on her face.

"What's up?" Evalycer asked.

"I'll tell you and your father about it at dinner," her mother said.

"I'm not in trouble?"

"Not this time."

Yes! Evalycer smiled as she followed her mother out to their vehicle.

After dinner that evening, her mother brought out slices of cake for everyone.

"What's the occasion?" her father asked, picking up his fork, ready to take a bite.

"I got that promotion I've been waiting for," her mother said, grinning.

"You did?" he exclaimed. "That's wonderful! Where to?"

"The Academy on Startia," her mother said.

Evalycer, happy just a moment ago, felt like she'd been dowsed with ice water.

Her mother noticed Evalycer's change in mood.

"What's wrong?"

"That means we have to move away," Evalycer said, her voice low.

"I'm afraid so," her mother said.

"It's a great opportunity for you mother to teach at Startia Academy," her father said.

"I know, but I'll have to leave my friends," she whined. "And what about Startia's Governor Atouu?"

Evalycer had heard people talking about the newly elected governor of Startia. She'd heard rumors about Atouu throwing his money around and buying his election, though no one could prove it. He had made several changes to his government, one being that once students graduated from the Academy, they had to serve a two-year internship in the government in some capacity.

"What about him?" her father asked.

"I want to be a pilot, not work for the government," she said firmly.

"Whether you want to be a pilot or not, it's required to work for the government. Maybe you'll learn something while working there that will help you as a pilot," he said.

"I doubt it," Evalycer mumbled, folding her arms across her chest.

"Next year, when you're old enough and you start drinking the Elixir, you can go to the Academy for free," her mother said.

"I guess that's one good thing," Evalycer said grumpily.

The Elixir gave people certain abilities depending on their genetic make-up, and Evalycer was eager to find out what abilities she'd have.

One more year to wait, she thought.

~~~~~~~~

A month later, they started the arduous task of packing for the move. Jaiy and Miranda left Evalycer alone to pack up her things while they packed up the rest of the items in their home. They knew that Evalycer was having a tough time adjusting to the idea of moving.

She'd had a hard time saying goodbye to her friends, since they'd been difficult for her to make. It had taken her a long time to change her attitude at school and learn to not say everything she thought out loud. But her father had been right three years ago. If she wanted to become a pilot, she'd have to get through school, and that meant learning to behave.

At school, her teacher gave her a going-away party in class, and her classmates hugged her, genuinely sad that she had to leave. Taniya, her best friend, cried at the end of the school day, knowing that Evalycer was leaving the next day.

"We can talk to each other on TechCall on our tablets," Evalycer said brightly.

"Every day?" Taniya asked.

"Sure," Evalycer agreed.

They'd hugged and Evalycer had left the school with tears in her eyes.

Now, Evalycer took her trunk out to the living room where her parents waited.

"Ready?" her mother asked.

"As I'll ever be, I guess," Evalycer replied.

Jaiy drove them to the nearby public spaceport. He'd already gotten their tickets two weeks earlier for a transport to Startia. Their things would be shipped there and arrive the next day. Evalycer took one last look around the spaceport before boarding the transport.

The trip to Startia would take a couple hours at light speed. While her parents read on their tablets, Evalycer looked out the window, deep in thought. If things didn't change, she'd have to work for the government when she graduated and possibly delay becoming a pilot.

They arrived at the bustling spaceport on Startia. Evalycer stayed with her mother while her father went to gather their belongings and find the desk for the company hired to take them to their new home. A loud screech made Evalycer turn her head sharply. She saw a man pulling a green cat-like creature in a cage, but the sounds the creature made reminded Evalycer of a bird she heard on Ennek, which made her miss her home all over again.

Her father returned fifteen minutes later, though it felt longer to Evalycer, who wanted to see their new city and home.

"We need to go outside and wait by the green sign for the transport company," he told his family.

Evalycer and her mother followed Jaiy through the spaceport, weaving around the people coming and going. While the clothing on Startia was similar in style, everyone wore more muted, earth-tone colors than they wore on Ennek. She looked down at her bright purple blouse and realized how much she stood out. She pulled her jacket across herself to cover her clothing.

They finally located the designated waiting place by the sign. It only took a few minutes for the driver to come. They climbed into the backseat and the driver sped away toward the capital city of Haven.

Evalycer watched the scenery out the window. The boxy homes and other buildings were so different from the rounded buildings of Ennek. The sharp corners gave the area a harsh look in Evalycer's opinion, not very welcoming.

The driver pulled up to a two-story complex in the middle of the city. The white, square-shaped building looked similar to the rest of the buildings on the street, the only variance being color. It was the middle of the day, so most everyone was either at work or school. Evalycer hoped someone her age lived in the area that she might be able to make friends with. The driver unloaded their luggage from the vehicle and helped the family take their items up to the building's entrance. Jaiy gave the man a tip of several credits.

"Have a good day," the driver said, and he drove off.

Jaiy put in the code to the building and the door swung open. Evalycer and her mother followed Jaiy into an elevator that took them up to the next floor. Her father looked at the apartment number again, and turned left. Their home was two units over from the elevator. He input the code to open the door and Evalycer went in straight away to look things over, pulling her trunk behind her.

"It smells funny," Evalycer remarked.

"It's probably been shut up for a few months," her mother said.

Leaving her trunk in the living area, Evalycer ventured down a hallway to the left. *It doesn't look like a home*, she thought, noticing the bare walls and a lack of most furniture. *I left my friends for this?*

The home came minimally furnished with some beds, a few chairs, and appliances, which would suffice until their own furniture came the next day.

She found two bedrooms and the bathroom. She went into one room that she hoped would be hers. It had a window set in one corner and a closet in the other. The bed in the room fit perfectly across from the window. It was smaller than the other room, so she figured her parents would take that one anyway.

She came out as her parents looked the place over.

"I found my room," she announced.

"Let's have a look," her mother said, and she and Jaiy followed Evalycer down the hallway to the bedrooms. Evalycer took her parents into the bedroom she'd chosen.

"Looks good," her mother said. "We'll take the other one."

Evalycer smiled and went to grab her trunk to take to her room.

The rest of their belongings arrived the next day. Evalycer set to work on her room and had it set up by the end of the night, her starscope aimed out her window. She always looked at the stars at night before going to bed. It relaxed her, seeing all the different systems and imagining going to them.

Evalycer sat and waited for her counselor to be free. Every student had to speak with a counselor during their final year of school, to discuss career options. She already knew what she wanted to do, and that was to be a pilot, but she had to get through her studies at the Academy first.

"Miss Nicholls?" the counselor called out.

Evalycer stood and walked into the office and sat down.

"Your instructors tell me you have an aptitude for mind-reading," the counselor stated.

"Yes, ma'am," Evalycer said.

Evalycer had been excited to drink the Elixir for the first time when she was fourteen. She had wanted to know what her abilities would be. When she drank the red liquid in her class for the first time, however, she didn't like the taste of it. The natural plant taste, similar to leafy greens and grass, had made her think it wasn't worth it. But once she saw her abilities forming—mind-reading, precognition, and strength—she made the effort every morning to drink it. Now, after drinking it for four years she didn't even notice the taste of it.

The counselor scanned the tablet she held in her hand, scrolling through pages. "Your grades are exemplary in all classes. Bit of an attitude, though."

"Yes, ma'am," Evalycer said, shifting nervously in her chair.

"All of your reprimands seem to be for speaking out of turn or talking back."

Evalycer wanted to say something, but figured she'd better not add insult to injury and stayed quiet.

"With your grades, are you sure you wouldn't want to work in the security field? You would be an asset to any place you worked for with your mind-reading abilities."

"I hadn't thought about it," Evalycer said. "I've always wanted to be a pilot. My father is in the security field and it seems boring to me. He likes it, but it's not for me."

"Perhaps a career in the military might be more exciting for you," the counselor suggested. "They have a security division, and you could be a pilot as well."

That piqued Evalycer's interest and she paid more attention.

"We don't have a military here, but it is required that all graduates work for the government in some capacity for two years after graduation. I could put in a good word for you to be able to work security as you train to be a pilot."

As quickly as she'd perked up, she slumped slightly and mulled this over. She'd known about the requirement to work for the government, but she had hoped that she could skip it somehow and serve it by training to be a pilot.

"Thank you, ma'am," Evalycer said. "I'd appreciate the help."

The counselor looked at her tablet again.

"You will need to learn to follow the rules and to not talk back," she told Evalycer. "I'd like to see improvement in that area. We'll revisit this in a couple of months. If you've improved, I'll make the recommendation."

I've got my work cut out for me, she thought, but just smiled and said, "Thank you, ma'am."

"You're welcome," the counselor said, putting her tablet down and standing to shake Evalycer's hand.

Evalycer left the office with lots to think about.

On her way to her next class, Evalycer found her friends Reina, Erik, and Theo waiting down the hall from the counselor's office. She'd met Reina and Theo in her new class when she first moved to Startia, and met Erik a year later at the Academy. It took some time, but Reina and Evalycer became close friends, though not as close as she and Taniya had been back on Ennek. Reina's quiet personality offset Evalycer's often sarcastic behavior.

"How'd it go?" Reina asked, tucking her brown hair behind her ear.

Evalycer shrugged. "About how I expected. 'You have good grades but watch your mouth'," she said. "She wants me to go into the security field, which is about as exciting as watching the rocks move on the ground."

"I have a friend who knows a way around working for the government," Theo said, leaning in to keep others from hearing.

"Really?" Evalycer asked, intrigued. She really didn't want to work for the government, but she would if it meant becoming a pilot. Maybe she wouldn't have to now.

"I'll talk to him and see if he'd be willing to come talk to us about it," Theo said.

~~~~~~~~~

Later that week, Evalycer, Erik, and Reina sat outside talking in the quad area of the Academy as Theo came up to them.

"It's all set," Theo told them.

"What's set?" Reina asked.

"My friend talking to us about other options to working for the government," Theo said.

"When?" Evalycer asked.

"Tomorrow afternoon," Theo said. "We'll meet him at the cantina after classes are done for the day."

When classes released the following day, Evalycer found Theo, Reina, and Erik outside waiting on the steps at the front of the Academy.

"Let's go," Theo said, and he led them down the street to one of the cantinas the students liked to spend time in after school.

The group went inside and Theo looked around for his friend. He spotted him across the room toward the back and motioned for his friends to follow.

"Hey, Theo," his friend said, shaking Theo's hand. "Please, have a seat."

The friends sat around the table. Evalycer noticed that Theo's friend was quite a few years older than they were. Gray strands ran through his otherwise brown hair, and he had the lines of someone who frowned rather than smiled.

"This is my friend Alexei," Theo told his friends.

They all introduced themselves, then Alexei got to business.

"Theo tells me that you all are not too keen on working for the government," Alexei started.

"Correct," Evalycer said. "I met with my counselor earlier this week and she's pushing me toward working security while I learn to be a pilot."

The rest of the friends had similar stories.

"Unfortunately, while you may be working security, you won't be able to pursue your interest in becoming a pilot," Alexei said. "Governor Atouu won't allow that to happen. You will spend all of your time working for him in some capacity. I know you've all heard about people resigning from the government and being replaced by people he knows."

The group nodded.

"Those are the people who gave him money for his campaign or people he's worked with in the past who share his ideals, which is not what is best for the people. That security job you'd have? You'd be spying on the people of Haven, making sure they all follow the rules."

"So what can we do?" Erik asked.

"You can't do anything to help until you graduate," Alexei said, pulling out his communicator. "I'll give you my contact

16

information, and once you *do* graduate, contact me. You can help me, and I'll help you."

Evalycer frowned. She wanted to do something now, not wait five months until graduation, and there was no way she was going to work for Atouu.

Alexei tapped an icon on his screen to transfer his contact info to the friends' communicators.

"I'm sorry this meeting doesn't help you now," Alexei said, looking at Evalycer. "But it lets me know that you're interested in change. It seems a long way off, but right now, you have to get through the Academy first and this time will actually fly by."

Evalycer looked at her comm to make sure she had received the contact information. She had.

"You mustn't tell anyone about this meeting," Alexei told them. "I trust Theo to use his discretion when talking to people about this, but right now, I don't know any of you, so please, do not talk about this. If Theo trusts you, I will trust you, but for now, I must ask for your silence."

"You got it," Evalycer said. Erik and Reina nodded in agreement.

"Excellent," Alexei said, standing to leave. "I look forward to visiting again in five months."

Alexei left the cantina.

"So, what do you think?" Theo asked.

"Can we trust him?" Erik asked. "He seemed like he knew what he was talking about but he's not going to turn us in for thinking about all this, is he?"

"I've known Alexei for two years now," Theo said. "I'm allowed to talk to people about this because my brother is in his group. He's not going to say anything to anyone about this."

The friends gathered up their things to leave. They went outside and Evalycer noticed Alexei standing across the street from the cantina, motioning for her to cross the street.

17

"Hey, guys, I'll see you later," she said to her friends. "I just remembered I gotta go pick up something for my dad down the street."

"See ya, Lees," Reina said, and the friends went up the street. Evalycer crossed once she knew they weren't going to look back.

"I wanted to talk to you a bit more," Alexei told her.

"What about?" she asked.

"Theo tells me you're at the top of the class for mind reading abilities."

"Yeah, so?"

"Your counselor may not know this, because the government tries to keep a lid on these things, but once your counselor mentions it to the government, they will try heavily to recruit you into the security team, which is a better name to call it than the 'spy team'," he said.

Evalycer smiled, amused. "Well, they will have a hard time getting me."

"Go along with whatever your counselor says, and even play along with the recruiters, but contact me the day you graduate. I think your talents will be better used by us than Atouu."

"I definitely will," Evalycer said, turning toward home.

Evalycer did as her counselor requested for the next three months. She made sure she didn't talk back to her instructors, and tried to keep the sarcasm in check while in class.

Her counselor called her in again to discuss her options.

"Are you still planning on becoming a pilot?" the counselor asked.

"Yes, ma'am," Evalycer said.

"I've looked over your grades and there is definitely improvement in the citizenship area. You've done well with keeping the back-talk to a minimum."

"Thank you," Evalycer replied.

"So, since I've seen improvement, I'll put in a recommendation for you to work security with the government for your requirement. I'll also see about getting you into a pilots program."

"That would be great," Evalycer said. "But I thought that I couldn't train to be a pilot while working for the government."

"Who told you that?"

"It was a few months ago, so I don't really remember," Evalycer said. She didn't want to let it out that she'd been talking to someone about changing the government, and quickly hid that info in case her counselor decided to read her mind.

"Well, they were misinformed. You can train as a pilot. In fact, some of the recruiters can possibly make it a package for you. You can work for the government during the day and train to be a pilot after work or on the weekends."

The more she had learned about Atouu's government since she lived on Startia the less she wanted to work for it. She wanted to make a difference, and knew there'd be no way to do that if she worked for Atouu. But if anything included a pilot's program, she would take that job, no matter what.

The counselor transferred an information packet from her tablet to Evalycer's.

"Talk it over with your parents," the counselor stated. "And come back and see me in a week. We'll get you going as soon as you graduate."

"Thank you, ma'am," Evalycer said.

At dinner that evening, Evalycer told her parents about the meeting with the counselor.

"She said she'd recommend me for security for my requirement," she told them. "She also said that she'd get me into the pilot program while I'm working there."

"Are you sure you want to work security? You know how exciting it is," her father teased.

"It's not really what I *want* to do," she told her father. "But she said with my mind reading ability, it's where I should go."

"I just don't think it will be what you or she thinks it is."

"I know. But if I can just stick it out while in the pilot program, it will be worth it."

"Working security for the government can be dangerous," her mother said. "I wish there was another direction you could take to get what you want. Couldn't you try for a desk job?"

"I'll ask, but the counselor is pretty sure that the recruiters will want me for security."

"Just keep your options open," her father said. "See what else comes your way from the government."

"I will."

Two days later, Evalycer found her message box filled with messages from recruiters. Most were from the security department, but some were from finance and others still from personnel. The recruiters from security all mentioned the pilot program, but only one from the other recruiters, in personnel, came with the offer of the pilot program. That one would only allow her to train in the pilot program on weekends. Most of the others offered training during the day after work.

We train pilots from the ground up, one message read, claiming to teach her everything while doing her service in the government.

Evalycer took her tablet to her parents to show them the messages and help her make a decision.

"I like the one from the personnel department," her mother said, looking over the tablet.

"Of course you do, Mother," Evalycer said with a grin. "But I can only train on the weekends. It will take me nearly three times as long to become a pilot."

Her father looked over the messages as well.

"There are a couple that look decent," he said. He tapped the tablet screen to highlight one entry. "This one says all you would have to do is help security read the minds of criminals as needed while studying to be a pilot."

Evalycer read it over. It *did* look promising. She'd be working with the security department when they brought someone in for questioning. She'd still be required to go out into the field, but she wouldn't be in any danger, and she would never be alone with any criminal or suspect. She could attend pilot school after she finished with her government duties for the day.

"I'll talk with my counselor tomorrow about it," she said. If she had to work for the government, at least she would get something in return for going against her principles.

At school the next day, Evalycer went to show her counselor the message to get her thoughts on it.

"It does sound perfect for you," the counselor said.

As the counselor read the message over carefully, Evalycer read her mind. Technically, students weren't supposed to read their instructor's minds, but Evalycer wanted to know if what her counselor said was also what she thought. Alexei had said that most of the instructors didn't know what went on in the government recruiting department, but Evalycer wanted to make sure.

21

Evalycer concentrated on the counselor, watching her as she read her mind. The counselor agreed that it would be good for Evalycer, and jokingly thought that it would be a good place for her sarcasm.

Evalycer snickered, then turned it into a cough. She didn't want to be caught reading the counselor's mind.

"We never had to go through all of this when we graduated," the counselor said aloud. "This is something that Governor Atouu started when he took office. He wants to make sure everyone knows what the government does, and maybe even get some of the students to stay on after their service is complete."

"Yes, ma'am," Evalycer said. "You had mentioned the military. I may go on to be a pilot there."

"You'd have to go to Darantha or Foridian or Monta Nesta to join, since we don't have a military here."

"That wouldn't be a problem for me. Maybe for my parents, though," Evalycer said, smiling.

Evalycer didn't read anything out of the ordinary from the counselor. The counselor seemed genuinely happy with Evalycer's choice, as she thought about Evalycer's grades and how well she learned everything.

"I'll make the arrangements," the counselor said.

Students couldn't make the decision for their service in the government without their counselor's and parents' permission. The counselor would contact Evalycer's parents to discuss it with them before contacting the recruiter's office.

"You should hear back from them in just over a week," the counselor told her.

Evalycer stood up. "Thank you so much," she said.

At lunch time, she found Erik and Reina talking together outside the cafeteria as they ate.

"Have you two thought about what Alexei said?" Evalycer asked quietly.

"We were just talking about that, actually," Erik said. "Reina's not so sure about joining him and going against the government."

Evalycer looked sharply at Reina. "Why not?" she asked.

"I just don't think it will do any good," Reina said. "It sounds very shady to me."

"What's worse—Atouu's government or this Alexei?" Erik asked angrily.

"My parents are very pro-Atouu. They like the idea of reading everyone's mind to keep them in line, as well as all grads serving in the government. They were so excited when my counselor suggested I work in the intelligence department."

With Reina's strengths of precognition and mind-reading, Evalycer knew she'd be very helpful in that department.

"You have to do what you think is right," Evalycer said, holding her hand up to Erik's protests. "How do *you* feel about Atouu?"

"He's vile," Reina said. "Not only does he take bribes, he's turning neighbor against neighbor, spying on each other."

"Then why work for him?" Erik asked.

"Maybe I can make a change from the inside," Reina said with a shrug.

"Good luck with that," Evalycer said. "Keep your options open. Just see what happens."

Using her telekinetic ability, Evalycer picked up a piece of fruit and grabbed it out of the air and popped it into her mouth.

Reina sighed. "Okay," she said, though Erik didn't look convinced. He didn't say much else while the girls' conversation turned toward graduation plans.

The end of the school year came and with it, graduation of all the fourth year students at the Academy. Evalycer fairly bounced with nervous excitement. While her parents and counselor thought she was going to work for the government, and she would for a while, she also had plans to bring about change.

She hadn't spoken with Alexei since the meeting they'd all had with him. Alexei had told her to contact him the day she graduated.

Did he mean before or after? she thought. She didn't think she'd have time after, so she contacted him right then. He answered on the second tone.

"It's Evalycer," she said.

"Good," Alexei said. "I've been waiting to hear from you. Today is the big day, isn't it?"

"Yes, sir," she said enthusiastically.

"Have you received your instructions for working for Atouu's office?"

Evalycer had received a packet via her tablet two days ago. In it, she had found instructions on how to check in and where to report. It had told her how to dress and what to bring with her.

"Yes," she told him.

"Follow those instructions carefully," Alexei told her. "It's important that they think you are with them one-hundred percent. Once you've established yourself there, we'll get started on our part. I think having you in the security department will be useful to us."

"Okay," she said.

"I'll meet with everyone over the weekend, so watch for my message."

"Will do!"

Alexei disconnected, and Evalycer dressed for the graduation. She had bought pink hair color a few days ago and decided to do it that day. She mixed the coloring chemicals together and brushed it onto her hair. Once done, she waited half an hour before showering.

As she finished dressing afterwards, her hair dried into bold pink streaks, in direct opposition to everything else on Startia. She looked at herself in the mirror and admired how the pink complimented her blonde hair.

Can't miss me in a crowd, she thought. She grabbed her dark blue graduation robe and went out to the living area where her parents waited for her.

"Ooh! I like the color," her mother said, picking up a strand of Evalycer's hair off her shoulder.

"Thanks," Evalycer said.

"Looks nice," her father said gruffly.

"What's wrong?" Evalycer asked.

"Oh, your father is just emotional," her mother said, smiling. "It's not every day your daughter graduates with honors and already has her future planned out."

More than you know, Evalycer thought. "Shall we go?' she said out loud.

"Yes," her mother said. She and her husband followed Evalycer out the door.

While her parents spoke to each other on the drive to the Academy, Evalycer sat quietly in the seat behind her parents. Her mind raced, thinking of everything that was about to happen in the upcoming weeks. She wasn't thrilled to be working at the government office, but would do it until things started to happen with Alexei's group. She was absolutely ecstatic to be in the pilot program and that would be the bright spot of her day.

They arrived at the Academy a few minutes later. As Evalycer got out of the vehicle, she said, "I'll meet you back here afterwards."

"Sounds good," her mother said. She and Jaiy both hugged Evalycer before turning to go to the auditorium for the ceremony.

Evalycer walked around the circular auditorium and went in the back door where she found Erik and Reina and the rest of the graduates. Before they had time to say anything other than hello, the staff ushered the friends into lines to walk out to their seats as the processional music drifted back to the graduates.

"I love your hair," Reina said as they walked.

"Thanks," Evalycer said. "I've been wanting to do this for a while. Now seemed like a good time."

As she walked through the door leading to the seats, Evalycer smiled at the banners hanging from the ceiling, congratulating the graduates. Flowers adorned the stage where they'd walk across to receive their diplomas. Members of the faculty sat in chairs across the back of the stage, her mother and father seated in the second row.

Once the graduates were seated, as the superintendent of the Academy spoke about career choices, the friends spoke amongst themselves.

"Did you contact Alexei?" Evalycer asked.

"I did," Erik said.

"I haven't yet," Reina said.

"You need to contact him," Erik whispered, although loud enough to be shushed by those around them.

"I'll do it after the ceremony," Reina assured her friends.

The speaking portion of the ceremony took almost an hour. They started to call up the graduates and announced their names and what they would be doing in the government.

It came time for Evalycer's row to go up. She followed Erik and Reina up to the podium, nearly pushing them in her excitement. She would finally be able to see all the places she had learned about as a child, studying the planets as much as she had.

"Evalycer Ophelia Nicholls," announced the superintendent. "Honors. Security and pilot program."

She took the diploma with a smile and shook hands with the superintendent, then walked across to the other side and went to her row. Once all of the students had returned to their row, they sat again.

Later at home after having a celebratory dinner with her parents, Evalycer looked at her instructions for beginning her service at the start of the week. She read over the dress requirements and found she didn't need to buy anything. Dark pants, a shirt or blouse that was easy to move in, and comfortable shoes. The security office would provide her with a jacket when she checked in. She also checked the information for the pilot program. She would report for instruction in the afternoon at the school near Atouu's offices. She could walk there once she was done with her government duties.

Evalycer awoke early for the start of her job at the government offices. She quickly dressed then went to eat breakfast with her parents.

"Today's the day," her mother said, smiling.

"Yes, it is," Evalycer replied. "I hear there is always a line to get in, so I want to get there a little early."

"I'm so proud of you, Lyci," her father said. "You're going to do well there, I think."

"I hope so," Evalycer said, though her idea of doing well and her parents' idea were as wide as the galaxy. She wasn't sure exactly what her part would be in Alexei's group, but she'd be ready for anything.

After she drank her Elixir, she grabbed her supplies and went out the door to make the trek to the public transportation. But what she saw outside of the house stopped her in her tracks. A small dark red land-rover with a pink bow on top of it sat in front of their home.

"Is this…mine?" Evalycer asked, spinning around to see her parents beaming.

"Yes!" her mother said. "We didn't want you to spend all your time on transportation getting to the office and back."

She ran to her parents and flung her arms around them both.

"Thank you!" she nearly shouted.

"Congratulations, Lyci," said her father.

She walked around the vehicle, dragging her hand over the shiny surface, feeling the smoothness of the metal. The land-rover would only hold two people, but Evalycer didn't care. She had her own vehicle! She stood back and looked at it again, noticing the four black wheels with their deep treads to get through sand or pavement.

Her father gave her the code to start it and told her how to lock it when she parked. She grabbed the bow off the top and tossed it into the vehicle, got in and input the code to start it. With a wave to her parents, she drove off toward the offices in the downtown district.

Evalycer drove into the parking area and found a parking spot. She set her code and walked up to the building and got in the short queue. As she stood there, the line grew longer, but didn't seem to move.

A few minutes later, people were slowly let into the building. Evalycer looked behind her and saw the line nearly stretched to the parking area. As she looked back, she saw Erik about twenty-five people behind herself. She waved and gestured that she'd wait for him once she got inside.

If this line will ever move, she thought.

Evalycer finally reached the doors. She pulled out her identification to show the clerk checking everyone in, then she had to submit to a mind-probe. A security officer took the long, wand-type unit and passed it over Evalycer's head. She had never seen anything like it, and figured it was how Atouu kept the employees in line while at work. Once past the mind-probe, she stood off to the side to wait for Erik.

"I guess we have that to look forward to every day?" he said as he walked up to her.

"Looks like it," she said. "Have you seen Reina?"

"No, but I got a message from her this morning saying she was running late."

"That won't make a good impression," Evalycer said.

"Hopefully she'll get here and in line and no one will notice," Erik said.

They walked across the lobby together toward the elevators.

"What floor are you on?" Erik asked

Evalycer looked at her tablet and found the information for her position. "Looks like…fourth floor."

"I'm on the fifth," he said.

The elevator doors opened and they followed the mass into the car. Everyone worked on a different level, so it stopped on all floors on the way up. At the fourth floor, the doors opened and Evalycer pushed her way out along with several others. She waved to Erik as the doors shut to continue its way upward.

Evalycer looked around at the signs on the walls, indicating the many offices on that floor.

"Where are you headed?" another girl asked. Evalycer recognized her from school.

"I'm going to the security offices," Evalycer told her.

"Me, too," said the girl.

They both looked at the signs and found the right direction.

"I'm Daleesa," said the brown-haired girl.

"Evalycer," Evalycer said, extending her hand.

Daleesa shook her hand. "I'm kind of nervous," she said.

"I don't know what to expect, either," Evalycer admitted.

They found the room they needed for their orientation and went inside. Other former students already filled most of the seats.

Evalycer spotted two chairs together toward the back and motioned Daleesa to follow her. They sat down and waited for the official start of the work day.

At exactly 0800, a man came into the room and the din of voices subsided.

"Good morning," he started. "I'm Mr. Ian Endock. I'm head of security. I'm glad to have all of you here today. I'm going to go over what is expected of you here, and then we'll hand out your jackets, and tell you where to go."

The orientation took about an hour. Evalycer listened, but knew that this was only a formality. She wasn't going to be there long.

When Mr. Endock finished the orientation, he had everyone form lines to receive their jackets for work. Evalycer stood four people back in line.

"Name?" asked the clerk when her turn came.

"Evalycer Nicholls," she said.

The clerk grabbed a jacket in her indicated size and handed it to her, and looked at her tablet again.

"Please report to Room 416," the clerk said.

Evalycer left the room and started down the hallway, Daleesa catching up a few minutes later.

"416?" Daleesa asked.

"Yep," Evalycer said.

They found the room and went inside. The open office held about twenty desks, all facing the same direction. The young women saw a line forming at one end and another intern motioned them over.

"We have to wait here for Mr. Endock to assign us a training partner," the young man said.

"Seems to be a lot of waiting in line here," Evalycer said.

It took another half an hour to get everyone assigned to a partner. Evalycer was assigned to a woman of about forty years old, and she waved to Daleesa, who was assigned to someone across the office. After introductions, the woman, Nita, gave Evalycer the run-down of what to expect.

"I'll be showing you the procedures and policies for the first couple of days," Nita began. "In a few weeks you'll get to do some interrogation work, but you'll just be there to assist, not to do the initial mind-reading. Also during that time, we'll assess your strengths and see what you can do. Any questions?"

"No, ma'am," Evalycer said.

"Good. Let's get started."

Nita took Evalycer to the library and showed her which books she would need to download to read. Nita pointed to the first in a series of policies, hit the button, and had Evalycer input her work code. A moment later, the book appeared on her tablet.

"I'm afraid it will be mostly reading for a few weeks," Nita told her. "But all new interns have to do this."

"Yes, ma'am," Evalycer agreed.

"I'll let you know when it's lunch time, otherwise I'll leave you to your studies," and Nita ran off to her desk.

Evalycer took her tablet to her desk that sat just in front of Nita's, facing toward the windows. She sat down and touched the screen to start reading.

Sometime later, Nita came to Evalycer's desk. "Ready for lunch?" Nita asked.

Evalycer hadn't realized she'd been reading for two hours straight. She rubbed her eyes and turned off her tablet.

"I'm famished," Evalycer said.

Nita took her down to the cafeteria and told her how it worked. They walked up to one of the ten automated food systems, where Nita showed Evalycer how to input a series of codes from the chart on the wall to get the meal of her choice. Evalycer put in a combination of codes and a moment later her meal popped into the compartment.

Erik came up behind them a moment later. "Hey, Lees," he said.

Nita stepped back and smiled. "I'll leave you to talk with your friends. See you back in the office in forty-five minutes." With that, she turned and walked to a table with the more senior employees.

"How's it going?" Erik asked.

"Lots of reading," Evalycer admitted. "She's got me reading all the policies and procedures of interrogating people."

"I think that's what we're all doing," Erik said. "Reina and I have a table in the corner if you want to eat with us."

Evalycer followed Erik to the table and sat down.

"I hate that we have to go through all this," Erik said.

"Me, too," Evalycer said. "But we've got to look like we're going to be here for the long haul." She suddenly sat up straight and glanced furtively around the cafeteria. "We need to be careful what we say and think here," she whispered, leaning in so her friends could hear. "Knowing this government, they could be reading our minds right now."

After work, Evalycer grabbed her bag with a change of clothes from her car before walking up the street to the building where she would be starting her training in the pilot program. Her vehicle would be safe at the government building for the few hours she would be receiving instruction.

She checked in at the front desk and they directed her to a room down the hallway. She stopped in the washroom to change out of her stiff government jacket and blouse into a comfortable shirt before heading to the indicated room.

"Are you Evalycer Nicholls?" the clerk asked.

"Yes, sir," Evalycer said.

"Good. I'll take your information and we'll get you set up in your classroom."

After getting the pertinent info, the clerk took Evalycer around the corner to the classroom. The class had already started, but the clerk took her to the instructor and transferred her data to his tablet, then with a wave, left the room.

"Evalycer Nicholls," the instructor read.

"Yes, sir," she replied.

"Take a seat and download the textbook to your tablet. We just started so you haven't missed much."

"Thank you, sir," Evalycer said.

She found an empty seat toward the back of the classroom, pulled out her tablet, found the correct textbook and downloaded it to her device.

The instructor, Mr. Kemp, continued with the class.

"After we've gone over a few things, I'll take you out to the hangar to look at the ships you'll be training in."

Excited voices rose up from the class. Mr. Kemp rapped his knuckles on the desk to bring it back to order.

"First things first. I need all of you to read over the survey I'm sending to you now, and fill it out. When everyone is finished, we'll go check out the ships."

Evalycer looked to her tablet and saw the survey pop open. It was the basic "getting to know you" inquiry that most instructors sent out.

She read it over carefully and answered the questions. When she got to the question of why she wanted to be a pilot, she tried not to sound too juvenile in her reply, since it had been her goal as a child to go to all the different planets and see the galaxy. She instead wrote down how she wanted to explore the galaxy and possibly join the military someday.

When everyone had finished, Mr. Kemp took them all down to the hangar bay to give them a tour of the hangar and the ships. As they entered the hangar, the trial pilots, as they were called now, looked around in awe at all the different fighters and other ships they would someday learn to pilot. Evalycer listened carefully as Mr. Kemp told them the capabilities of each ship and what they were used for.

"Most of the ships all have the same basic technology," he said. "Some may have subtle differences in start-up sequence, but all are pretty much the same."

Mr. Kemp took each student into one of the fighter ships and showed them the console and how everything worked. When Evalycer's turn came, she entered the ship with the wonder of a child seeing the stars for the first time.

Evalycer had so many questions that she and Mr. Kemp were in the ship for ten minutes.

"You are certainly full of curiosity," he laughed.

"Can't learn if I don't ask questions," Evalycer said.

"That is true," he said. "After class today, come see me and you can ask more questions."

He pointed to a cargo ship, larger than the fighters, as Evalycer guessed a cargo ship would be.

"This beauty runs a little differently," Mr. Kemp told them.

Mr. Kemp led the way into the ship. Everyone fit easily into the main cockpit and hold area. The cockpit had more instrumentation than the fighters.

"Most of the instruments are the same," he told them. "But the console also shows what's in the cargo hold and what the weight is. This console here," he said, pointing to a screen on the pilot's side. "Has all the controls for life support, weapons…"

"Weapons?" Evalycer asked.

Why does a cargo ship need weapons?

"Yes," he said, smiling. "We'll go down to the weapons station in a few moments."

After they finished in the cockpit, Mr. Kemp took the trial pilots down the hallway to the weapons station.

"The weapons station is here mostly for defense," he started. "You wouldn't normally send a cargo ship into a battle. The weapons have to be charged before use, so if you need to defend yourself, you'd better be prepared."

He showed them a few more things on the ship, then took them back to the classroom.

Evalycer thought about each of the ships she'd seen. The fighter ships interested her the most, though the cargo ship with the weapons station also intrigued her.

"Now that we're back in class," Mr. Kemp said, bringing Evalycer back to the present. "You will study how each ships works and will be able to diagnose and repair anything that may happen on the ship. You'll be able to use the ship and its features easily, and learn to take care of the ship to keep it in top form."

By the time Mr. Kemp had gone over everything, school had ended. Evalycer picked up her tablet and bag and started to follow everyone out of the classroom, but remembered Mr. Kemp told her to see him after class.

"Your counselor from the Academy sent me a note earlier, telling me about your desire to join the military," he said.

"It's an option I'm looking into," Evalycer said.

"She also said you graduated with honors."

"I did," she said, and wondered where this was going.

"I think you'll do well in this program. You looked like you caught on quickly to the overview of the ships."

Evalycer had a few questions to ask about the fighter ship and the cargo ship.

Half an hour later, her curiosity assuaged for now, she thanked Mr. Kemp for his time and walked back to the government building to get her vehicle to drive home.

Her mother was just finishing up with dinner preparation when Evalycer got home.

"How was work and how was the pilot program?" her mother asked.

"Work was okay," she said. "I'm not real excited about it. It's a lot of reading right now. But the pilot program was great! Mr. Kemp, the instructor, showed us all the ships we're going to learn about. Some reading to do, but not as much as the government job. Mr. Kemp thinks I have a knack for learning about the ships."

"Did you talk his ear off?"

"Nooo..." Evalycer said sheepishly.

Her mother laughed. "I knew you would. Your father will be home in just a few minutes, so why don't you get ready for dinner?"

"I'll be back in a minute," Evalycer said, and she headed to her room to put her things down and get everything set up for her homework.

Evalycer told her parents more about the pilot program over dinner. Jaiy wasn't surprised how inquisitive she'd been about the ships.

"And Mr. Kemp said that if I ace the pilot program, I can enter the military as a sergeant," she told her parents.

"Excellent," her mother said. "I know you've got the intelligence to do this, if this is what you want."

"I'm still deciding, but I think it may work out well."

After dinner, Evalycer went to her room to work on her homework. It wasn't a lot, but she wanted to make sure she did whatever she could to finish the program at the top of the class. Just as she finished the last question about the different ships, her communicator buzzed.

"Can you come to a meeting?" Alexei asked.

"Now?" Evalycer asked.

"Yes. It won't last for very long. Meet us at the Mill Street Bar right away."

Evalycer looked at her watch. It was nearly 2200 and she wanted to go to bed. She sighed and said, "I'll be there."

She changed into comfortable clothes and went out to the living area where her parents were watching holovision.

"I'm meeting my friends for a little get-together to talk about our work day today," she told them.

"You won't be late, will you?" her father asked.

"No, maybe half an hour to an hour at the most."

"See you in a while," her mother said.

Evalycer arrived at the bar a few minutes later. Though a bar in name, it was more of a hangout for young people, as techno music played over the sound system and groups of young adults gathered around the tables. She spotted Alexei and Erik and a few more people at the back in the corner.

"What's up?" Evalycer asked as she sat down next to Erik. She noticed that Reina wasn't there.

"This is just an informal meeting to see how everyone is doing on their first day with the government jobs."

"Lots of reading," Erik said with a laugh.

"Yes!" Evalycer agreed. "Too much reading."

"As you read see if you notice anything that will help us take down Atouu," Alexei said. "We need him out of office as soon as possible. He's corrupt and is just going to run this

39

government into the ground. Those of you with mind-reading abilities, try to use your abilities to read what's going on there."

"I'm not sure how helpful Nita will be," Evalycer giggled.

"You never know," Alexei said. "Just keep your ears, eyes, and minds open to anything that might help us. We're going to start meeting once a week until things start coming together, then we'll meet more often. I have a small warehouse in the industrial district where we will meet from now on. I'll send directions to your comms before the next meeting."

Alexei next spoke to them all about what the leaders expected of them.

"Being at the meetings is essential," he told them. "As we'll be discussing progress and making new assignments as needed. There will be some training involved as assignments are made, so we need you all there, every time. If not, you'd better have a damned good excuse."

Evalycer hoped that they would be able to make the changes needed to make the government work for the people instead of the people working for the government.

Atouu had made promises during his campaign that he never intended to keep and then, once elected, made other laws without going through the proper channels. In the time that she'd lived on Startia, Evalycer had seen changes where some people reported their neighbors for minor issues such as having opposing views of the governor.

Evalycer realized she'd have to start hiding things if she continued with this group. If neighbors were turning on neighbors for that, she'd have to be careful.

After Evalycer got back home, she contacted Reina.

"You weren't at the meeting tonight," Evalycer said.

"I told Alexei that I couldn't make it because my family was having dinner with my sister who just got back from Foridian," Reina said.

"How did Alexei take it?"

"He wasn't happy, but I had to go to dinner. I *think* he understood," Reina said, unsure.

"I'll see you at lunch tomorrow," Evalycer said, and turned off the comm.

The next day, Evalycer read more about the policies of working for the government. As interns, even though they were being paid, they were not allowed to talk to the press about anything.

That's good, I don't want to talk to them, anyway.

They were also not allowed to voice their opinions publicly about anything the government does. While this would fall under the policy of not speaking to the press, it also comprised the security department.

"Nita?" Evalycer said as she turned her chair to face the older woman.

"Yes?"

"I have a question." She got up and went to show Nita what she'd just read. "What does this mean? Does this mean I'm going to hear things that are security related? Will I have to keep secrets?"

"Oh, no, dear," Nita said with a smile. "It's just in case you rise in the ranks here *into* security. Right now, it's nothing to worry about."

Evalycer relaxed. "Good. I really don't want to get that far up here."

"Getting that far up takes about five years. Some people like this job, others don't. I have that level of security, but I prefer working down here in the file room. Makes life easier."

"Thank you, ma'am," Evalycer said, sitting back at her desk.

After lunch with Reina, Evalycer went into the book file room to download more files to read. While in there, she got distracted by all the titles in the room and just kept reading them until someone clearing their throat brought her back to the present.

"What are you doing down that far?"

Another office worker stood in the aisle, hands on her hips, looking like Evalycer had broken her best dish.

"I'm sorry," Evalycer said. "I just started reading all the titles and didn't realize I'd gone so far."

The woman softened her stance somewhat, though still glared at Evalycer.

"Make sure you don't do that again," the woman said. "There are some files in here that interns are not allowed to read until they receive intern security clearance."

"I do apologize," Evalycer said, sliding past the woman and walking quickly back to her desk.

Evalycer did well in the day's pilot lessons. She had read everything that had been required and then some. Mr. Kemp was impressed.

"I may have to give you private lessons if you keep this up," he said.

A week passed and Evalycer got the information for the next meeting. It was a little further than the bar they'd had it in the previous week. She hoped it wouldn't be a long meeting. She had to tell her parents she was meeting a study group and didn't know when she'd be home.

Evalycer found the well-lit warehouse. She looked around before getting out of her rover, though if anyone tried anything, she'd deck them. Her strength ability wasn't the best, but she could pack a punch if needed.

She hit the button to open the door of the warehouse and heard the motors grind and engage. The door slid open with a loud scrape. She stepped inside and walked down the dim hallway as the door scraped shut again. Evalycer smelled a strong scent of dampness mixed with rusty metal and wood. She heard voices and followed the sound to the main warehouse where the meeting would take place.

The dimly-lit room made it hard to find Erik and Reina in the group. A few lights had been placed around one end of the room where several rows of chairs had been set up, facing a monitor two meters high. The chilly air of the vast warehouse made Evalycer shiver slightly. As she walked toward the group gathered in the lighted area, she saw Erik and again looked for Reina.

"I think Reina has decided this is too much for her," Erik said crossly.

"She won't say anything to anyone, will she?" Evalycer asked. She didn't want her parents to know about this just yet.

"I don't think so," Erik said. "I ate lunch with her today at work and she seemed to be okay with you and me being in the group."

"She must've felt guilty hiding this from her pro-Atouu parents," Evalycer stated.

Evalycer noticed that most of the older members of the group had weapons. That made her a little uneasy. Would she be required to carry a weapon of some sort? And why did they have weapons in the first place?

Her thoughts were interrupted as Alexei stood up and called the meeting to order and everyone took a seat.

"We have a few new recruits to introduce," Alexei said. "Erik, Evalycer, Max, and Jack."

The four of them waved from where they sat. Evalycer was glad she didn't have to stand up and say anything. While she didn't mind talking in small groups, the thought of talking to fifty people, even briefly, gave her a knot in her stomach.

The meeting that night was mostly to introduce the new members. Alexei told them the meetings would be at the same time and place as this meeting, once a week. Evalycer would figure out something to tell her parents when she left for these meetings.

Chapter Nine—Promotion

After her first two weeks, Evalycer was called into the security office to speak with one of the interrogators.

"I've been looking over all the intern's transcripts from school," he started. "And you have very good marks in mind reading and telekinesis."

"Thank you, sir," Evalycer said.

"We can definitely use you in our office here, if you're interested."

"Sure."

Evalycer wasn't interested in working the security office for herself. She knew she'd probably hate it. But it would be beneficial for her and the group if she could learn certain things about what they do in security and let the group know.

"Have you finished all the reading of policies with Nita?" he asked.

"I'm done with the policies, but not the other modules."

"I'll send a message to her to find out for sure, and then we'll have you start working in this office next week."

Evalycer went to that night's meeting with the group to let Alexei know this latest development.

"That will help us tremendously," Alexei said with a smile. "Be cautious, however. They will make you spy on everyone. You seem like an intelligent girl and I don't think you really want to do that."

"Absolutely not," Evalycer agreed.

"Make them think you're doing your job. Give them just enough info to keep them happy."

"I will."

The following week, Evalycer found herself assigned to the security office, though at a junior level. She was given second level intern security clearance, which enabled her to read some private files and modules, but mostly she would be involved with interrogations. The security office's idea of interrogations, however, was to go out and read the minds of people in the city where crimes were being committed. Evalycer wasn't keen on that, but she'd somehow figure out a way to give the office what they wanted.

She'd seen the security agent, Jax, around the security floor, talking to some of the advisors in the office where Evalycer worked. Jax had spent a lot of time talking to Nita, and she figured she'd be going out into the field with Jax soon.

She went out with Jax that morning to the market area where people were shopping, meeting people, and going about their daily business. Nothing looked out of the ordinary.

"Atouu wants to make sure that everyone is following his laws," Jax told her. "He wants it made clear that anyone who doesn't follow his policies is going to be dealt with."

"What does that mean, 'dealt with'?" Evalycer asked.

"Nothing we have to worry about," he said. "We just bring them in to interrogate them if we find anything amiss. Easy job, really."

Evalycer didn't like the sound of that, but she'd keep her thoughts to herself for now, hiding her misgivings as much as she could. She didn't relish the thought of having to be duplicitous, but she'd do almost anything to get Atouu out of power, even if she had to compromise some of her beliefs for the time being.

While out in the field, Jax and Evalycer read the thoughts of a group they'd been watching.

"What do you see?" he asked her.

Evalycer concentrated on one man there. He was speaking to another man. She read his mind and she saw that he was planning a surprise party for his wife. She giggled.

"I really don't think we need to worry about him," she said to Jax. "Surprise parties are not illegal."

"Keep reading," Jax told her. "He's up to something."

She sighed and concentrated on the man again. She still only saw his plans for the party. She continued to concentrate, and then she saw that the other man there gave him something. Reading his mind, she found that the man had given his friend the mood-enhancing drug Upzidrine. He planned on giving it to his wife so she'd enjoy the party.

"He gave the guy Upzidrine," Evalycer said.

"Yes, he did," Jax said, pulling out his binders.

"Upzidrine isn't illegal," she protested.

"I know, but to give to someone without their knowledge or consent is."

She followed Jax across the street and held back a bit as Jax took over the job.

"Sir, we need you to come with us," Jax said, as he pulled out his badge to show to both men.

"I haven't done anything wrong," the first man said.

"Not yet. We need you to come in for questioning." Jax turned to the other man who gave him the drug. "You can go."

The other man took off as Jax put the binders on the man. Evalycer followed Jax as he took the man to their vehicle and put him in the back.

"See how easy that is?"

Evalycer did indeed see how easy it was to bring someone in who wasn't even guilty of anything. It made her uncomfortable, but she'd have to get used to it for now.

Jax drove them back to their office building where they would interrogate the man. He and Evalycer got out of the vehicle and Jax grabbed the man's arm and helped him out of the back.

Still holding his arm, he led the man to the interrogation room, reached into the man's front pocket of his pants and found the small bag of the drug. He tossed it onto the table and took the binders off the man.

"Please sit," Jax said, indicating the chair across from him. The man sat and looked around nervously.

Evalycer felt as nervous as the man looked, her stomach doing flip-flops. She had no idea what to expect. This was supposed to be a training session, but she wondered what would happen. A moment later the door opened and another interrogator came in.

"You can watch from the corner, but pay attention," Jax whispered to her as the head of security, Ian Endock, took the seat next to Jax.

Evalycer knew of Ian's reputation. His mind-reading skills were above par, and she knew he had a quick temper. He could be a rough interrogator for criminals to deal with. He'd been the interrogator giving them instruction at their orientation their first day there. With his slicked back dark hair and permanent scowl, he could be intimidating.

Evalycer nodded and happily went to the corner to observe. She wanted nothing to do with this, since this guy hadn't committed a crime yet.

"Tell me," Ian started, looking at the man. He picked up the bag and shook it in the man's face. "What were you going to do with the Upzidrine?"

"I-I-I was g-going to use it for myself," the man stuttered. "I'm throwing a surprise party for my wife and wanted to have fun."

Evalycer could see Jax concentrating on the man and his thoughts. She did so as well, and could see the man was lying.

"What do you think, Jax?" Ian asked. "Should we take him on his word?"

The man shifted in his chair.

"He wouldn't *lie* to us," Jax said. "He knows we can find out the truth very easily without him having to say a word."

Evalycer kept reading the man's thoughts. He'd gotten in trouble with security before. It was a minor violation, but according to Atouu's laws, breaking the law or almost breaking a law and then lying about it would be grounds to jail him overnight. His dilemma now was if he admitted to wanting to give it to his wife, would they give him more jail time for that?

"Okay," the man said. "It was for my wife for her party. She's been depressed lately and I wanted to help her enjoy the party."

Ian and Jax looked at each other. "Seems he *was* about to commit a crime," Ian stated. "Giving the drug to an unsuspecting person is illegal, you know," he said, turning back to the man.

"I was just trying to help her," the man whined, his eyes darting around. He focused on Evalycer, looking for sympathy. Ian turned to look at her, too, then turned back to Jax.

"Who is this?" Ian asked.

"This is my trainee, Evalycer Nicholls," Jax explained. "It's her first day out in the field."

"Well, Evalycer," Ian said, facing the man again. "What do you think we should do with him?"

Evalycer didn't want to get the man in trouble for *thinking* about committing a crime, but she needed to be trusted by the government. They were going to jail him no matter what she said, which only slightly abated her misgivings. She stated the facts.

"He was about to commit a crime," she said, her voice steady. "I read his mind and he was going to give it to his wife without her knowledge. That is illegal."

Ian smiled and turned to Jax.

"I like her!" Ian enthused, slapping the table. "Make sure she does more field work with you to get trained up. The last trainee we had was too wishy-washy."

Ian turned back to the man.

"We're going to have to hold you overnight for this."

The man lowered his head and swore. Evalycer felt bad for the man, and this made her resolve to make the changes needed to get Atouu out of office. Thinking about committing a crime wasn't the same as going through with it, but for now, she had to play by the rules.

"Jax, take him down to the holding area and process him. Take Evalycer with you. It'll be a good learning experience for her."

Ian stood up, shook Jax's hand, and turned to Evalycer.

"Keep up the good work," he said as he shook her hand.

"Yes, sir," she said.

Ian left the room with the evidence as Jax put the binders back on the man and he and Evalycer took him down two floors in the elevator to the holding area. She watched as Jax filled out the forms on his tablet. It took about fifteen minutes to get everything taken care of, then she followed Jax as he took the man to his holding cell.

"We'll let you contact your wife in about an hour," Jax told him as he hit the button to shut the cell door. The man sat down on the cot in the cell. Head in his hands, he looked defeated and scared.

Evalycer took a long look at the man before following Jax back upstairs to the offices. This was Atouu's government— arresting people before they committed a crime, or for even thinking about committing a crime. It made Evalycer nauseous.

"Good work, by the way," Jax said, turning toward her as they ascended the stairs. "Ian hardly likes anyone. He hates when people don't know their own mind. You answered him confidently and truthfully. You may have a new friend here."

Wonderful, she thought sarcastically.

Evalycer wasn't sure how she felt about the praise. She wanted to do well and be trusted, but she hated, absolutely hated what she had to do to get it. She was going to have to stop caring about her feelings and anyone else's to get this job done.

Evalycer rushed home to put her work and training items away and to change before going out again.

"Aren't you going to stay for dinner?" her mother asked, concerned.

"No," Evalycer said. "I'll eat on the way to my meeting."

"You certainly have a lot of meetings," her father remarked.

"Yeah," Evalycer said. "I've got lots to learn."

She hoped that her parents wouldn't ask any more questions after that. They didn't, and she waved to them as she went out the door. She wasn't exactly lying to them. There was lots to learn, just not for her work or career.

She arrived at the meeting warehouse a few moments later.

"'Bout time, Nicholls," Alexei said.

"Sorry, sir," Evalycer said. "It's hard to get home after pilot training to change then get all the way back here."

Evalycer found Erik at his usual spot in the back.

"You didn't miss anything," Erik told her. "He's just stressed because this is taking so long to do."

Evalycer listened as Alexei continued speaking.

"I need those of you who are working in the government building to start reading minds there to find out anything that we can use to put an end to Atouu's reign. Find out where and when he will be places, what his routine is. Our spotters are doing a great job but we need to know what goes on inside as well."

Evalycer had never really had any chance to read anyone's mind while working in the government offices. After all the reading they'd done the first couple of weeks, her job there was to read minds of the citizens of Startia. She didn't like it.

The only time she had any chance to read anyone's minds was when she went with Jax when they booked someone. As Jax entered the info into the computer, Evalycer tried reading the minds of the people in the security unit there. Not knowing who was who there, however, she didn't get much information from them. If Alexei wanted to know anything, he'd have to find someone in Atouu's offices on the top floors to find what they needed.

The bright spot of her day was going to pilot school after work. Evalycer found joy in learning all she could about becoming a pilot, and she was learning it all at a much faster pace than the rest of her class. It was the only place she felt she could truly be herself, besides home, though even at home she had to be on her guard about what she said.

On a night where she didn't have to go to the meeting with Alexei's group, she and Erik met at a cantina for drinks and to talk.

"It's been forever since we've been able to just sit and have a conversation that's not related to our extra-curricular activities," Erik said with a smile.

"Yes, it has," Evalycer said, sipping her soft drink.

"How are things at work?" he asked.

"I hate it," she stated. She lowered her voice. "I hate that we have to read people's minds and take them in for interrogation if they even look like they're about to commit a crime."

She told him about her first day of training and the subsequent couple of days, where she helped bring in a few more people committing questionable activities.

"I have to hide all my feelings about this every morning because of the mind probe they perform on us. I guess it's good practice for me, since I'm in this group."

An up tempo song played and Erik pulled Evalycer up to dance. Erik and Evalycer held hands as they danced. He spun her around and caught her as he leaned her over his arm in a dip. Erik held her in that dip for a few moments. Evalycer smiled at him, looking into his eyes. Erik bent down and gently kissed her lips. She stood up and looked at him, and returned the kiss. He pulled her close as they kissed deeper, more passionately in the middle of the dance floor. The song ended, but they continued to stand out on the floor, kissing, holding each other.

She'd always liked Erik, but all through the Academy he never seemed to be interested in anything other than friendship. She had a crush on him when she first met him, but then realized he wasn't interested, so she looked at other boys in her class. She'd dated a few, but nothing more than going to teenager hang-out spots. It got boring hanging out with the same kids every other night.

The sound of cheers brought them out of their momentary bliss. They looked around and laughed as the crowd watched them on the floor. Erik waved and Evalycer gave an exaggerated curtsy, then they laughed as they went back to their table.

"Well, that kind of broke the mood," Evalycer remarked.

"Who said it can't be fixed?" Erik asked. "You want to go to my place?"

"That's totally not a pick-up line."

Erik laughed.

"We don't have to do anything if you don't want to," he said. "I just want to get out of here."

"Sure," she said.

They walked out of the cantina holding hands and went around the corner to Erik's apartment building. He punched in his code to open the door. It slid open and they walked in, the door sliding shut again behind them. They walked up two flights of stairs to his apartment on the third floor. He input another code to open his door.

"Lights," he commanded and the lights came on, showing quite a few projects laying around in various stages of completion. The projects filled up more space than the furniture, as there was only a couch, table, and holovision unit in the bright blue room.

"Are all these projects for work?" she asked.

Erik worked in the electronics department at the government building.

"Most are," Erik said from his kitchen. "These are just the prototypes that I'm working on. The real ones I obviously can't take home. These are just to figure out how to get them to fit together. The electronics will come in later." He pulled out some glasses. "Do you want something to drink?"

"Sure."

Erik pulled out a few different bottles.

"We have water—ha ha—Red Aged, Jenubrian Gold ale, or Pelonsa Reserve."

Despite being of legal drinking age for several months, Evalycer had never really had any desire to try alcohol. Until now. Her life was becoming more stressful as her involvement with the group went on.

"How about the Pelonsa Reserve," she said, not knowing anything about any of the drinks.

"A fine choice," Erik said. He poured them each a glass of the dark green beverage and brought them out to the living room where Evalycer stood.

"Cheers!" he said, and they clinked the glasses and drank.

The Reserve had a fruity taste to it, then it warmed as it went down.

"I think I like this," she said.

"Be careful, it's really strong stuff. It's actually outlawed on Darantha because of its alcohol content."

Erik hadn't been kidding. After one glass, Evalycer felt more relaxed than she'd been in a long time. Erik poured himself another glass, but Evalycer didn't want or need anymore, feeling light-headed already.

She leaned over and kissed Erik. He turned to return the kiss, pushing his hands up into her long hair. She felt Erik's tongue push past her lips as he deepened his kiss, making her heart flutter. She grabbed hold of his shirt, trying to pull him even closer to her as she lay back on the couch, Erik moving with her, on top of her now. He stopped kissing her for a moment to look into her eyes.

"What's wrong?" she asked breathlessly.

"I just want to make sure that this is what you want," he whispered.

"I want you," she said, biting her lower lip.

He pulled off his shirt, and began kissing Evalycer in earnest. She let him unbutton her shirt and pull it off. He covered her face with soft kisses, moving to her neck, then her chest. She ran her hands through his blond hair as he did so, then guided him back to her lips again.

He stopped to unbuckle his belt and slide his pants down his legs, and she did the same. As they lay naked on the couch, Erik smoothed Evalycer's hair from her face. Evalycer smiled, and that was all it took for Erik to kiss her more eagerly, running his right hand down her arm, stopping to caress her breast. She moaned in his ear, and that encouraged him on. He wedged his knee between her legs and gently entered her, her hands on his hips, pulling him into her.

Evalycer never knew how happy someone could feel until that moment. As they moved together, she felt every muscle release the stress from her body, and she felt totally free from everything. She thought about nothing but that moment, feeling Erik on her and inside her. His weight on her was comforting, like she'd never be in danger.

An hour later, they lay breathless on the couch, Erik lying on his left side beside her, stroking her shoulder.

"That was amazing," Evalycer said softly. "I didn't know it would feel so good."

"That was your first time?" Erik asked, surprised.

Evalycer nodded.

He stopped stroking her.

"I didn't realize," Erik said, raising up on his arm.

Evalycer giggled. "It's okay. I'm glad it was with you."

Chapter Eleven—Progress

Several weeks went by without much opportunity to make any advancement on learning about Atouu and his weekly agenda, and Alexei wanted to move on the government soon.

"Those of you working in the security department need to step it up and get going," Alexei started. "It's been three months and no new intel from there."

Evalycer frowned. She wasn't the only one working in the security department, but felt Alexei's anger was directed at her. She'd been trying to get something for him, but Jax always wanted her to go with him on another training session and bring people in to interrogate.

With all the field work she was doing, however, she was getting experience in reading people's minds, and also learning to hide her thoughts. The mind probe each morning made her nervous, as she didn't know how well she'd hidden her thoughts. If they found out anything about Alexei's group, her friends would be in trouble and possibly in danger. She especially feared for Erik, whom she had gotten even closer to these past few weeks. The two of them worked in the same unit in the faction, as Evalycer started to call their group. They got together whenever they could for lunch or dinner or fun, sometimes going out with Reina and her boyfriend.

Evalycer decided that she'd have to take things into her own hands at work. Alexei wanted to know more about Atouu's schedule. The schedule wasn't a secret, but it was hard to find out about beforehand. Usually it was posted the day of Atouu's engagement, making it hard to let the faction know.

Alexei gave Evalycer instructions on how to navigate their computer system at the offices. It wasn't hard, but it could be risky to have that information during the morning mind probe. She had gotten very adept at hiding what needed to be kept from everyone, but it still made her nervous to have the information in her head.

At work the next day, Jax met Evalycer in the hallway.

"Ian wants you to stay in the office today and get some of your modules done," Jax told her. Despite her good work out in the field, she'd fallen behind in learning more about the policies. Jax reluctantly left her at the office.

Evalycer sat down at her desk and turned on her computer. Nita came by to see her a few moments later. "Jax finally left you to your studies?" she joked.

"Yes," Evalycer said. "I'd tried to get him to let me stay before now, but he wanted me out in the field."

"Rumor has it you're very good out in the field. Ian doesn't like anyone new, and he likes you. Just continue on from where you left off," Nita said, indicating the computer. "You can probably get all caught up by the end of the week if you hustle."

Evalycer smiled as Nita left her to her studies. She logged into her next lesson, and started reading.

After an hour, Evalycer looked around furtively to see who was still in the office. There were a few people there, all facing their computer screens, and Nita had gone downstairs for a meeting. Evalycer opened another window on her computer, and followed Alexei's instructions to hack into the system without raising suspicion. As an intern, any of the senior members there could see what she was doing on her computer, as an icon would pop up on their computer. Alexei had given her a code to put in to turn that feature off. She input the code, logged onto an online shopping site, and waited.

Nothing happened. No one stood up, no one called. She smiled, and continued onto the page that had Atouu's schedule, and again waited. When nothing happened still, she quickly found the file and inserted the small drive Alexei had given her to copy the schedule. The entire month had been scheduled, and Evalycer made a few quick keystrokes and had it copied in under a minute. She pulled the drive back out, shoved it into her pocket, and logged out of the site before closing the window.

After work, she rushed over to pilot school to take her test in the fighter that afternoon. She'd done the work and Mr. Kemp had spent some time with her after lessons to show her more of the ship's abilities. She'd be the first in her class to take the test.

Mr. Kemp spent about an hour getting the class started on their next lesson, then another instructor came in to take over the class while he took Evalycer out for her test.

Evalycer followed Mr. Kemp into the smaller fighter. He hit a button to close the hatch, and they proceeded into the cockpit.

"You can take the pilot's chair," he said with a grin.

Evalycer happily sat down in the chair. She rubbed the arm rests and ran her fingers over the controller, imagining flying the ship. Mr. Kemp let her take a moment to enjoy the experience, then got down to business.

"Your headset is there," he said, pointing to her left side. She grabbed the headset from its hook and put it on her head, adjusting the communicator attached to it so it would be in front of her mouth. The ear piece fit her ear perfectly.

"Can you hear me?" he asked into the comm.

"Yes," she said.

"Good, and I can hear you. Okay, we are now starting the test. What's the first thing you need to do? Just do it; you don't need to tell me anything. I'll let you know if it's wrong."

Evalycer took a deep breath and let it out slowly. She quickly looked over the console and located the switch to turn it on. The gauges and readouts appeared. She looked them over, committing them to memory. The fuel looked good, cockpit pressure was good. They'd already established the radio worked. She started the pre-flight checklist.

"Radio is good," she started. "Fuel is full. What's the electronics status?" she asked Mr. Kemp, who was acting as her co-pilot.

Mr. Kemp looked over his console. A yellow light flashed.

"Electronics are slow to come up," he said.

She tapped the light to make sure it wasn't an error. The light continued to blink.

"I can fix that," she said, and she took off her headset and went back to the circuit panels and removed one of the covers. She looked over the schematic on the cover, then looked into the compartment. She wiggled a few wires and circuits, and found the loose circuit. She pushed it on with her finger.

"That took care of it," Mr. Kemp called to her.

Evalycer replaced the cover and went back to her chair.

"Loose wire," she told him, putting the headset back on.

She finished the pre-flight checklist and started the engines. They roared to life, and she listened to them to make sure they were running correctly. After looking over the console once more to make sure all was running well, she was ready to go.

"This is test flight one-one-nine-five, requesting permission to leave the hangar bay," she said into the comm.

"Permission granted," came the reply. "Good luck!"

"Thank you, ma'am," she said with a smile.

She turned to Mr. Kemp, who nodded, and they both nudged their controller forward. The ship started to move, and Evalycer's heart nearly burst with excitement. Using her Elixir abilities as well as the controller to guide the ship, she cleared the hangar bay and flew out into space.

"Well done," Mr. Kemp said. "You passed that part of the test with flying colors, if you'll forgive the pun."

"Thank you, sir," she said.

"Now I'll have you perform some maneuvers to see what you're capable of out here."

Mr. Kemp gave her instructions on what to do. Evalycer performed each skill quickly and effortlessly. Flying using her abilities came naturally to her.

Half an hour later, they landed back in the hangar bay. Evalycer performed the end of flight sequence, and they disembarked the ship. Mr. Kemp didn't say anything as they walked back to the classroom, and Evalycer didn't ask any questions. She felt confident that she had passed, but waited for Mr. Kemp to say one way or the other.

Evalycer sat in her seat while Mr. Kemp put in the grades for her test, then he stood up and addressed the class.

"I just finished the first pilot's test with Evalycer Nicholls. I'm here to tell you that she passed all parts of the test. Congratulations!"

The students cheered and clapped for her. Evalycer smiled, and waved to the class.

"Thank you, sir," she said to Mr. Kemp.

Once the cheers died down, Mr. Kemp continued. "She handled every aspect properly, even the error that came up on the console and knew how to fix it. Well done!"

After class, Evalycer drove home and ran into her home to tell her parents the news.

"I passed my first pilot's test!" she exclaimed, throwing her bag on the floor.

"I knew you would," her mother said with a smile.

"Congratulations," her father said, giving her a squeeze.

"What happens next?" her mother asked.

"Well, I have more training and studying to do," Evalycer said. "Then another test in the cargo ship."

"That's wonderful, Lyci!" her mother said.

Evalycer was so excited that she almost forgot about her meeting with the faction that night. She ate quickly and changed her clothes. As she went to the door, she remembered the drive in the pocket of her other clothes. She went back to her room to retrieve the drive, then left.

She arrived a few minutes later, just as Alexei called the meeting to order. She slid into her seat beside Erik and squeezed his hand.

"I passed my test," she whispered excitedly.

"That's fantastic!" he said, and he kissed her quickly as Alexei called the meeting to order.

Alexei went over what they had learned recently about Atouu's latest antics within the government. Evalycer of course knew all this since she worked there. There were only a few new developments.

During the break, Evalycer left Erik to speak with Alexei.

"I got it," she told him.

"Got what?" he asked, not paying much attention as he scanned his tablet.

"Atouu's schedule. For the next month."

Alexei turned his head sharply to look at her.

"You got it?"

Evalycer pulled out the drive and held it out to him.

He grabbed it and shoved it into the port on the side of his tablet and tapped a few keys. The schedule came up. He scrolled down the schedule, then back up again.

"This is excellent! Just what we needed."

He called everyone back to order.

"We've got Atouu's schedule," he announced.

Everyone cheered, and Erik came over to Evalycer.

"You've had a very busy day," he said with a grin.

"It was fairly easy, and luckily Jax let me stay in the office today. I'm behind in learning the policies there."

Theo came up to the friends with a grin on his face.

"You can thank me for Jax letting you stay in the office today," Theo said.

"What do you mean?" Evalycer asked, confused.

"Well, I knew you couldn't get what we needed if you kept going out into the field, so I hung out by the security offices today and placed some thoughts in Jax's head."

"You can do that?" she asked, surprised at his ability.

"Yep! With practice, it's pretty easy," Theo said.

"Awesome," Erik said.

"Yeah, thanks," Evalycer said. She didn't know that mind manipulation was even possible. She'd have to work on that sometime.

Now that the faction had Atouu's schedule, things started happening at each meeting. Alexei assigned everyone to a group, and gave the group a job to do. Evalycer had been assigned to the group that would take care of the offices when everything was put into motion.

It took a lot of convincing by Erik to get Evalycer on board with what needed to be done. She wasn't keen on using violence to do any of this.

"You had to know it would come down to this," Erik said as they discussed what they would do.

"I just didn't think I'd be so involved with it," she said. "I just wanted to take Atouu down, not hurt people. I can't jeopardize my pilot training."

Erik took Evalycer aside.

"I'll see what I can do to make your part in this minimal. I know you're working hard to become a pilot, and I'm so proud of you."

"Thank you," she whispered.

He kissed her slowly, then they returned to their group.

Their unit's part in this would be to secure the floor where they would be taking hostages. Atouu would be part of those hostages, so they needed to secure the area from those who would come to save Atouu. Evalycer didn't want to hurt anyone, but Alexei assured her it would just be the Stun feature on the blasters or using their abilities to render them unconscious. She could live with that.

Evalycer prepared for work the next morning. Afraid that they would find out what the faction had planned, she took a long time clearing her mind. She didn't know what either the government or Alexei would do to her if they found out.

She arrived at work and stood in line at the building entrance for the probe. She saw Erik running over to her. He pulled her out of line, ignoring her protests.

"Here," he said, slapping a small bag into her right hand.

"What's this?" she asked, looking carefully at the package.

"It's a probe-blocker," he told her. "We need to start taking these before we go in, otherwise they'll know what we're doing."

"I don't know," she said. "I'm pretty good at blocking their probes."

"Alexei doesn't want to take chances. He doesn't trust Atouu and wouldn't put it past his office to find a way to dig deeper into our minds. It's already an invasion of our privacy to read our minds, and frankly, I'm sick of it."

"So am I," she said firmly. It put a lot of stress on her each morning to try to hide anything that could hinder their efforts. "Is this safe? I'm not going to be drooling later at my desk, am I?"

Erik laughed.

"It's perfectly fine to take. I tried it yesterday and it was okay. I did have a headache for about an hour, but that was it."

Evalycer looked at the package again. *Drastic measures*, she thought, and she opened it and shook a tablet out into her hand.

"Take one each morning," Erik told her. "It's a little close right now, but it should work today with your skill for hiding things."

Evalycer put the tablet in her mouth and swallowed a few times to get it to go down without water. She and Erik got back in line. The line was shorter now, but she'd be a few minutes late. As they got closer to the entrance, she could feel everything fading away in her head, except for things that had happened that morning at home. They both passed the mind probe.

"I'll see you at lunch?" Erik asked.

"Sure," Evalycer said, and she walked quickly to her office.

Nita looked at the clock. "You're normally not late," she said. "Everything okay?"

"Yes," Evalycer said. "My friend pulled me out of line to ask me on a date. Sorry I'm late because of that."

She didn't like lying to Nita. Nita was a good person who just happened to work at the government offices. Her part in this was just to train people and take care of the forms.

"Well, I hope you said 'Yes'," Nita replied.

"I did," Evalycer said, blushing.

"Good! Then all is forgiven," Nita said with a smile, and went back to her work.

Jax came by a moment later.

"How many more modules do you have to learn?" he asked.

"I think about five more," Evalycer told him.

"So about a weeks' worth?"

"Yes."

"I want to get you back into the field as soon as possible. They won't let me take you out again until you're finished with the mods."

Evalycer decided right then that she just might purposely take a little longer to get through the mods.

"I'll see how much I can get done this week. Hopefully they're not too hard."

"You're a smart girl, you'll be fine." With that, he turned and left her to her studies.

Her encounter with Jax and his wanting her back in the field to read the minds of Startia's citizens made her resolve to do whatever it took to bring down Atouu's government.

"We're going to take the cargo ship out today," Mr. Kemp told his class. He looked to Evalycer. "You'll be my co-pilot."

Evalycer's heart skipped a beat.

"Seriously?" she exclaimed.

"I'm pretty confident you can handle it," he said with a wink.

The class followed Mr. Kemp into the cargo ship and gathered around the cockpit console. He gave everyone a quick refresher on where everything could be found within the ship and what to expect once airborne. The class watched and took notes as Mr. Kemp and Evalycer went over the pre-flight checklist. He read off everything and Evalycer checked it off or fixed it if it wasn't ready.

He had the class strap themselves into the seats while he requested permission to leave the hangar bay.

Once airborne, Mr. Kemp talked with the class about flying a cargo ship, how it was different from the smaller space craft.

"We're flying empty right now," Mr. Kemp told them. "The ship handles a little differently once it's laden with cargo. You have to make sure the cargo is strapped in so it doesn't shift around as you fly. We'll do another flight in a couple days with some cargo, and you can feel even as passengers how differently it handles."

Mr. Kemp and Evalycer performed a few simple maneuvers with the cargo ship, mostly to let Evalycer get a sense of how it handled and to give the rest of the class the experience. Mr. Kemp let a few other students take the co-pilot's seat for a few moments, and they all commented on how heavy it felt.

Evalycer took the co-pilot's seat back and they headed back to the hangar bay. Mr. Kemp and Evalycer shut down the engines and followed the class out of the ship.

Back in the classroom, Mr. Kemp went over more about the cargo ship. They would take the ship up again at the end of the week with cargo in it, then the following week they would have tests for both ships.

Evalycer looked forward to her pilot classes, and eagerly awaited the cargo ship test. The classes were the best part her day, after having to deal with her government internship and then the faction in the evening. The only other thing she looked forward to was being with Erik.

The faction met more frequently after they had gotten the month's schedule. Things needed to be planned out, and Alexei wanted to make sure everything ran smoothly down to the second.

"Listen up!" Alexei started in on the meeting. "We've decided on a day three weeks from today to take over the government."

Cheers arose from the group, but Evalycer felt a knot form in her stomach. Although she would be happy to get rid of this government, she wasn't excited about having to take hostages. At least her part in it would only be to keep people from entering the floor.

Alexei waved his hands to hush the group. "That means we need to take everything to the next level. Get your units in order and get your plans ready. I want this to go off without any issues."

Evalycer's unit needed to start planning how to keep the floor safe and keep people from coming up.

"We need to block the exits," Erik started to say. "I can get the key to turn off the elevator, but we'll need people watching the stairs. Evalycer can take one side and Dell the other. Alexei and his group will take the hostages and run the demands." Erik looked at Evalycer standing next to him. "It will soon be over," he said quietly to her.

Evalycer had told Erik many times how much she hated this scheme, but would do what her conscience allowed her to do.

Erik always took that into consideration, and it made her happy to know that Erik watched out for her.

After the meeting, Evalycer sat in the hallway, waiting for Erik to gather up his things from the meeting room. She let her mind wander a bit, finding Alexei and his group in the next room.

Atouu won't know what's hit him, she heard in her head as she read Alexei's mind. *By the time he realizes, it will be too late.*

Evalycer turned her head toward the room, trying harder to concentrate on Alexei. She could see in her mind that he was reading over the plans she had given him.

Yes, that will work well, she read.

She caught her breath, then looked around to make sure no one was around to notice her shock. Erik came out a moment later from another room.

"Ready?" he asked.

She took a deep breath, letting it out quickly to steady herself.

"Sure," she said, and she followed him out to the street as they walked to his apartment a few blocks away.

They arrived at Erik's apartment only a few minutes later. Without asking, Erik poured Evalycer and himself each a glass of Pelonsa Reserve. He handed a glass to Evalycer, who took a sip.

"What's wrong?" Erik asked.

"When do *we* get *our* help from Alexei?" she asked.

"What do you mean?" Erik asked.

"Well, when we first joined this group, he said if we help him, he'd help us. I guess I'm just feeling a little used by him as well as the government."

"He *is* helping us by getting Atouu out of office," Erik replied. "It's going to take some time, Lees."

Evalycer sighed. She'd been feeling more and more disillusioned by this whole "take out Atouu" business.

"I just thought it'd be different. Theo said Alexei knew a way around working for the government, yet here we are. I thought

I'd be out of the government offices by now. I don't like having to read people's minds out on the streets."

Erik sat next to Evalycer on the couch and put his arm around her shoulders, pulling her closer to him. She lay her head on his shoulder

"Give it time. I think once we get Atouu out of office, Alexei will make good on his promise to us."

Evalycer didn't share Erik's outlook, but said nothing more about it.

Awakening at home the next morning, Evalycer happily took the probe-blocking tablets. She wasn't sure what she'd read in Alexei's mind last night, but didn't want to have to explain it or stress about hiding it. She wanted to make sure she knew all the facts before deciding what to do.

Alexei possibly had been doing nothing more than planning to take hostages. That was the plan that *she* knew after all, and what they had planned for in her unit with Erik. She'd have to read Alexei's mind at the next meeting, going against her beliefs about reading unsuspecting people's minds. If she was going to act on what Alexei might be doing, she needed to do it.

Evalycer passed the mind-probe that morning and went to her desk to work on more of the modules she needed to learn.

The modules she had to learn took longer than she anticipated. The one she was now reading took a day and a half to finish. Her mind would wander to pilot school and then to the faction with each chapter she read. Jax wasn't happy about it taking so long.

"I want to get you back in the field, Evalycer," Jax stated. "I know you got through all the policies, but you gotta get through these other modules quickly. Ian's been on my ass to get you back. He thinks you're going to be an asset to this department."

Evalycer didn't like the sound of that. She'd heard a few things around the department about Ian. He was a hard-nosed security officer who didn't care how he got criminals off the street, even minor ones like the man they'd put in a cell her first day out in the field. That man had been released the next day, but she heard that his wife had threatened to leave him if that happened again. Luckily, that was all she'd threatened. Evalycer would have to get a thicker skin if anything worse happened.

"I should be done with them by the middle of next week," she assured Jax.

"Okay," he said. "Don't take any longer or I'll have to see what the hold-up is."

Evalycer swore under her breath as Jax left. She'd have to get the modules done and not lollygag anymore.

At pilot school that evening, Mr. Kemp took the class up in the cargo ship again, with cargo in it as promised. Everyone in the class had finally passed their first pilot's test, and a few were ready for the cargo training. Mr. Kemp had Evalycer sit in the co-pilot's chair first. They went over a few things as the class watched and listened, then they strapped themselves into their seats as they took the ship out into space.

Evalycer could feel the difference between the empty ship they'd taken up before and the cargo-laden ship they flew now. It handled differently.

"The artificial gravity in the ship does make a difference," Mr. Kemp stated. "The cargo makes the ship heavier, so it handles differently. Not much, but enough to notice."

Mr. Kemp performed some maneuvers so Evalycer could really feel the difference. After a few minutes Mr. Kemp had Evalycer switch with another student who was ready for his cargo training.

Afterwards, Evalycer and the other student compared notes on the cargo ship.

"Did it feel different when you landed?" Evalycer asked.

"It did," he said. "I felt a little drag on it, kind of sluggish."

"That's how it felt taking off, too," she told him. "But nothing I couldn't compensate for and handle."

After pilot training, Evalycer went home to change and eat a quick dinner before heading to the faction meeting. She sat next to Erik and kissed him quickly as Alexei called the meeting to order.

Alexei went over everyone's part again in the takeover. It was now two weeks away. Evalycer normally didn't get nervous about things, but this made her uneasy.

As everyone split up into their units, Alexei and his group went into the office and shut the door. Erik talked to his group, but Evalycer wasn't listening as she stared at the floor, trying to concentrate on the minds of the people in the office. She couldn't hear what they were saying, but their minds were quite clear to read. *I guess their probe-blockers have worn off*, she thought.

"Hey, Lees," Erik said, bringing her thoughts back to the meeting. "Where'd ya go?"

She shook her head to clear it.

"Sorry, Erik," she said. "I was thinking about my training today," she lied.

"I wanted to make sure you knew how to use a blaster. Have you held one before?"

"Actually, no. The only weapon I've ever used was my wit and charm."

Erik and the group laughed.

"Okay, you'll join my group to learn how to use it. It's not hard."

Evalycer quickly cleared her head of what she'd been doing, hiding what she'd seen as she followed Erik and two others to a room that had been set up for combat training.

"It's pretty much just point and squeeze the trigger," Erik told the group. He held the blaster out to show them the safety feature was engaged, then showed them how to change it from Kill to Stun. "We want you to have it on Stun only," he said, winking at Evalycer. "We're not killing anyone, we just want to keep them at bay."

He gave the weapon to Evalycer.

"Disengage the safety feature, then point it at that target over there. Whenever you feel comfortable, pull the trigger."

The blaster felt heavy in her hands, but not uncomfortably so. She made sure it was set to Stun, switched off the safety feature, and took aim at the target. She took a deep breath and held it as she squeezed the trigger. Even with the Stun feature it left a mark on the target, dead-center.

"Wow!" Erik said. "You're a natural."

Evalycer smiled, pleased that she had done well on her first try.

"Switch it to Kill, and try again," Erick encouraged.

Evalycer pushed the button to Kill, took aim again, and hit the target, just slightly off-center this time.

"Excellent," Erik said. "Alexei will be pleased with that."

Evalycer switched the blaster back to Stun, engaged the safety feature, and gave it back to Erik with a smile.

The other two also did well with the blaster, hitting their mark near the center of the target.

"I don't think you'll need any more training unless you want it," Erik told his group.

After the meeting, Erik invited Evalycer to his apartment for a nightcap. Evalycer happily went with Erik to spend some time with him. They hadn't been able to get together much lately, because Erik had to work on his projects for the government.

"Pelonsa Reserve?" he asked as they went into his kitchen.

"Please," she said.

It'd been a hell of a stressful day. Jax on her back to get back out into the field, and learning to use that blaster, though she had to admit that part had excited her.

Erik handed Evalycer a glass of the Reserve, then clinked her glass with his.

"Great day today," he said, and he sipped his drink.

Evalycer smiled, and took a long drink from her glass. She had to put aside what she'd seen earlier so Erik wouldn't be suspicious, and took a moment as she drank to hide her thoughts.

"I didn't realize how easy blasters were to use," she said now.

"Yeah, they don't require a lot of knowledge."

"How did you learn to use one?" she asked.

73

"My dad taught me," Erik told her. "He was an officer with the Aknor Intelligence Taskforce when I was growing up. He taught me how to use one when I was fifteen years old."

"*Was* an officer?"

"He was killed a couple of years ago, transporting a prisoner to another holding facility. At least the other officers killed the son of a bitch as he tried to escape."

"I'm sorry," Evalycer said softly.

"So, after I'm done with this government job and taking down Atouu, I'm going to apply to the Taskforce."

"Back on Aknor?"

"Most likely, though I'll weigh my options."

Evalycer looked at the time and set down her half-finished glass of Reserve.

"I gotta go," she said. "If I'm going to get my homework done before tomorrow's class."

Erik walked her down the street to her vehicle.

"Maybe tomorrow we can have a real date again?" he asked, eyebrows raised.

"Definitely," she said. "I'll see you after I get home from class."

Erik kissed her softly, then opened the door of her vehicle to let her in. He shut the door and Evalycer drove home.

Once at home, she went to her room to concentrate on what she'd read in Alexei's and the other men's minds. As she sat on her bed, legs folded, she relaxed and cleared her mind to bring everything into focus to see the future. Scenes formed in her mind as she concentrated on the faction. The mission wasn't what Alexei had told everyone. While they told the members they'd only be taking hostages, they were really planning to kill Atouu while everyone did their job of keeping people out of the offices. The more Evalycer remembered what she'd read of their minds, the more it terrified her. They were going to disable the Stun feature on the blasters, so anyone they shot at would be killed.

She breathed in sharply as she came back to the present, her eyes wide.

I can't let this happen, she thought. *How can I stop this?*

At work the next day, Evalycer tried to forget what she'd read in Alexei's mind by finishing up her modules. Jax wanted her to go out in the field with him that day, even though she wasn't finished.

"You can finish tomorrow," he told her. "Ian wants you out there with me because you're above the rest in reading minds."

Damn it, she thought. *Why'd I have to be so good?*

One other reason she didn't want to do it is because she was afraid Jax would read her mind without her knowledge, just as they were doing to the citizens of Startia.

Although laws were in place regarding mind-reading, Atouu's government didn't much follow the laws. He wanted to make sure that people did as they were told. You stayed out of trouble if you did everything by the book, followed the laws, and kept your head down. As one who hardly ever followed the rules to the letter, it was the worst place for Evalycer to be at the moment. By working at the government offices and doing what she's told, she had kept out of trouble, but was afraid at some point Jax or Ian, or really anyone in the offices, would read her mind without her knowing. She'd become very skilled at hiding her thoughts, but wondered if it was enough. She'd have to act quickly once she had more information about what was going to happen.

Jax took her to an area close to where the faction met. She tried not to show that she recognized the area, though Erik's apartment was in the neighborhood, so *if* that question came up, that was her answer. She wasn't going to volunteer any info, however. Jax didn't need to know about her private life.

"There's been a lot of activity in this area recently," Jax said as they drove around the streets.

"Like what?" she asked, trying hard to keep her voice level.

"Mostly kids wreaking havoc on businesses, but there's also been some activity in some empty warehouses. It's mostly at night, but I'm hoping we can read minds and stop anything before it happens."

Evalycer's heart skipped a beat, but she said nothing and hoped that Jax wouldn't pursue the warehouse concerns. Luckily he turned down another street away from the building where the faction held their meetings.

She breathed easy again as they turned the corner and drove another kilometer to get closer to the schools. Jax pulled over and parked. The sun cast longer shadows as the schools released for the day.

"We'll wait here until the kids start passing us, then we can read their minds," Jax stated.

It made Evalycer uncomfortable to sit there and wait, knowing they were doing something illegal in the eyes of the law. But of course, it's what Atouu wanted, so they did it. She pushed her feelings about it aside and concentrated on the kids as they started to walk past on the opposite side of the street.

"What do you see?" Jax asked.

"So far, nothing out of the ordinary stuff kids think about after school," she said. "Kids worrying about their tests, someone wanting to ask out a girl, another not wanting to go home to an empty house."

"We'll keep reading. They'll come by eventually."

They read the kids' minds for another fifteen minutes before they saw a group of four boys who were jumping around and pushing each other, just messing around.

"Those kids there," Jax said. "Read their minds."

Evalycer stared at the kids, concentrating on their thoughts. She did read that they were planning to do something that night to one of the businesses down the street.

"They're going to break into the hardware store down the street tonight," she said.

"We'll alert the authorities and they can arrest them," Jax said, and he called it in.

They drove around a bit more, mostly just to make sure there were no thoughts from anyone about doing anything illegal, then they went back to the office.

Ian greeted them as they got back to their floor.

"Good work out there, you two," he said, looking at Evalycer. "We'll get those kids tonight and make sure they know what they're doing is wrong."

"Thank you, sir," Evalycer said, but she didn't feel thankful. She wanted to get out of the office as quickly as she could.

Ironically, as if he'd read her mind, Jax told her, "You can leave early today. You can finish your last module tomorrow morning, then we'll do more field work."

"Thanks, Jax," she said, and she quickly picked up her belongings and left the building.

She got to her pilot training quickly and asked if she could just sit in the cockpit of the cargo ship to study more of its features.

"I think you probably know everything there is to know," Mr. Kemp said. "But sure, I'll be happy to open it for you."

They walked to the hangar and Mr. Kemp let her into the ship. She sat in the pilot's chair, but didn't need to look anything over. She just wanted a quiet place to sit and collect her thoughts regarding the day. It made her sick to even think about what she'd had to do. She didn't like compromising her principles to do this government job, but it was the only way to get Atouu out of office.

During pilot training, Mr. Kemp took the class out to the hangar again and had two more students take the controls of the cargo ship. Mr. Kemp let Evalycer be the co-pilot, under his watchful eye. She had advanced faster than the other students, and Mr. Kemp had confidence in her skills, but since she was a student, he had to keep watch.

The students and Evalycer had no problems with the flight instruction. At the end of class, Mr. Kemp had some news for her.

"I've spoken with the head of the department," he began. "I've asked permission for you to take your pilot's license test next week. They've agreed."

"Really?" she exclaimed. "That'd be awesome!"

"You've easily learned everything you can from me. I think you're ready. I know you use your abilities to fly, which a lot of the other students haven't figured out how to do yet. That gives you the advantage."

"Thank you, sir," she said, shaking Mr. Kemp's hand.

"In the meantime, make sure you study as much as you can. The test isn't easy, and because I've asked to have you tested early, they will put you to the hazard, I'm sure. You've gotten through this course in four months whereas it takes others six."

"I'll study all weekend! See you!"

When she arrived home for dinner, her parents noticed her smile.

"I haven't seen that smile in a while," Jaiy said. "What's up?"

"Mr. Kemp arranged for me to take my pilot's license test next week" she said excitedly.

"Already? Is he sure you're ready?" her mother asked.

"Yes. Apparently I'm far ahead of everyone else in the class. He let me be the co-pilot today for the other students. It's all I've wanted to do, be a pilot."

"I haven't seen you this happy in a long time, so I'm glad this is happening for you," her father said.

Evalycer's excitement abated after dinner, as she got ready to go to her faction meeting. She'd started telling her parents that she was meeting friends, which wasn't an actual lie. Her friends *were* there, they were just doing other things.

"When do we get to meet this Erik?" her mother asked as Evalycer started for the door.

"Soon," she said. She was actually nervous to have Erik over, concerned he'd say something about their meetings. "I'll see if he can come over this weekend."

"Good," her father said. "I want to make sure this guy is good enough for you."

Evalycer laughed.

"Will anyone be good enough for me, Daddy?" she asked with a laugh.

"Probably not," he joked.

She got to the meeting place early with the intention of trying to read Alexei's mind again. She didn't feel bad about reading his mind without his permission, as she needed to know what she was getting into. Killing innocent people wasn't what she signed up for.

Evalycer sat in the hallway, under the pretense of reading on her tablet. Following Atouu's laws that she firmly disagreed with, she concentrated on the closed door where Alexei and his men were talking. She read that they were still planning to kill Atouu, but they were making changes to how to achieve that. They would talk about it at the meeting.

Erik came up to her a moment later.

"You're here early," he said, kissing her quickly on the cheek.

"Jax let me leave work early," she told him. "Then I didn't have to stay for the entire class at school, so I got home in time to eat with my family and leave there without rushing. I have something exciting to tell you!"

"What's that?"

"I'm going to take my pilot's license test next week!"

"Wow! That's great!" he said, and he picked her up and spun her around before kissing her lips.

"If I decide to join the military, that will give me a step up on the others."

"That's fantastic," he said, smiling.

Alexei and his group came out of the office. "We'll start the meeting in a few minutes," he said, then saw Evalycer there. "You're here on time for once."

"Only because of a happy chain of events," she told him.

They followed Alexei and his group into the meeting hall. Once everyone had arrived, he started the meeting.

"I have new ideas for everyone," Alexei started. "I'll call up the heads of the units and fill them in, then they can let you all know."

Erik left the room with Alexei and the other unit leaders. They were gone for a long time. Evalycer tried to read what was going on, but it was hard in a roomful of people. Erik came back a few minutes later with a solemn expression on his face. Evalycer didn't like the looks of it at all.

Erik took his unit to a separate room, as did the other leaders.

"I've got some news," Erik said. He sighed, and continued. "Our unit is no longer going to secure the floor where the hostages will be taken."

Evalycer's heart sank. She knew what he would say next and didn't want to hear it.

"We will now be in charge of blowing up the offices."

This change upset Evalycer, and by the comments made, a few of the other members as well. This was *not* what she signed up to do. The rest seemed happy about the change of events.

"Alexei has asked me to request that anyone who is not up to the task, excuse yourself now," Erik stated.

Three people got up and walked out. Evalycer wanted to join them, but she had to keep playing the part now. She had given the faction Atouu's schedule, knew what they were planning, and needed to find out more.

Erik looked at her and smiled briefly.

"Those of you who have stayed, thank you. Here's what we have to do now."

Erik went over what they were supposed to do now. He tried to keep Evalycer's part in it to a minimum, but she would still have to show up.

After the meeting, Evalycer went to Erik's apartment again. She wasn't happy with this change and wanted to just forget about it.

After two glasses of Pelonsa Reserve, her inhibitions gone, she kissed Erik passionately, pulling at his shirt to take it off. He finished taking it off, and unzipped her blouse. He caressed her breasts, kissing her neck.

She didn't want to feel anything except Erik's love. She ran her hands over his back and shoulders, feeling every definition of his muscles. She started to pull his pants over his buttocks, and he kicked them off. He unbuttoned her pants and pulled them off, tempering his kisses. He smoothed her hair from her face, looking into her eyes. She could see the love he had for her and smiled.

"I love you," she whispered.

"I love you," he said.

He kissed her slowly, running his right hand down her side, down to her thigh, then up between her legs. Once she was ready, he slowly entered her. They moved slowly at first, then quickened the pace. She hadn't wanted to think about anything, and she wasn't except for that moment. Erik held her close as they climaxed, Evalycer holding Erik's hand and watching his face. When the last ripples left their bodies, Erik collapsed on her, burying his face in her neck.

"Oh God, that was great," she breathed.

"Yes it was," Erik said, smiling.

They lay together in his bed and fell asleep for an hour. When Evalycer woke up, it surprised her to see it was so late. Her communicator beeped continuously.

She pulled it out quickly and saw her mother's code displayed. She hit the button to answer.

"Hi, mom," she said. Erik stirred next to her. "I'm at Erik's place. I fell asleep I was so tired…I'll be on my way home soon…okay, bye."

She put her communicator back and turned to see Erik awake. He reached out and rubbed her back. She lay down again.

"I didn't realize it was so late," she said.

Erik looked at the clock.

"It's not that late, but later than you've been here before."

Evalycer realized that she couldn't drive in her state of inebriation.

"I'm gonna be in trouble if I don't leave here soon."

Erik got up, pulled on his pants, and went into his bathroom for a moment. He came out with a bottle.

"Take this," he said, handing her the bottle.

"Toxi-tabs," she read.

"Take one and in a few minutes, you'll be safe to drive home."

Evalycer opened the bottle, shook out a tablet, and swallowed it down. She could feel everything becoming clear again.

"Wow, that works fast," she said.

"I've had my fair share of benders, so I keep them so I can drive afterwards."

"Thanks."

She gathered up her clothes and put them on. Erik walked her to her vehicle parked outside his building. She leaned back against her vehicle and Erik stood close in front of her.

"Thanks for a fun night," he whispered.

She smiled.

"Thanks for making me forget about things tonight. I love you."

"I love you, too."

Erik opened the door for her. She got in, started the engine, and drove home.

Chapter Sixteen—Pilot's Test

Evalycer spent the weekend studying for her pilot's license test. She had her father quiz her from her notes and the text book on her tablet until she knew the answers forward and backward. She studied the readouts on her tablet of the ship's consoles she'd be tested in. She couldn't have been more prepared for her test when she arrived at the school after work at the start of the week.

Mr. Kemp walked with Evalycer to the hangar where they met the licensing director, Captain Jon Monroe.

"Nice to meet you," Captain Monroe said, shaking Evalycer's hand. "I'll be administering the written test and the cockpit test. The written test will take about twenty minutes, then the flying portion will take half an hour. Are you ready?"

"I am," she said with a smile.

"Good. Sit down at the desk and we'll get started."

"Good luck," Mr. Kemp said. He gave her a pat on the back, and left.

Evalycer sat down at the indicated desk. Captain Monroe uploaded the test to Evalycer's tablet. She set her tablet to "test" mode, which blocked any search engines, and started the test.

Fifteen minutes later, she finished the test, but checked over her answers during the final five minutes. Sure she had answered everything accurately, she raised her hand.

"All done?" Captain Monroe asked.

"Yes, sir," she said.

She uploaded her test to his tablet, and sat with her hands folded on the desk as Captain Monroe went over her answers.

"Well done," he said finally. "You only missed one question, and that question could have gone either way."

"I knew I should have picked the other answer," Evalycer admonished herself.

"Truth be told, that's the one I missed, too." He stood up and she did the same. "Let's get you up in the air. Lieutenant Langston will accompany us in the fighter for this portion of the test."

Lieutenant Daria Langston was waiting at the fighter for them. She shook Evalycer's hand, then followed them into the ship.

"First, we'll test in this ship, then the cargo ship," Captain Monroe said.

Evalycer took the pilot's seat, Captain Monroe the co-pilot's, and Lieutenant Langston the jump seat behind Captain Monroe.

"Whenever you're ready, go ahead and start," he told her.

Evalycer had a hard time keeping the fluttering in her stomach at bay as she looked over the console to familiarize herself with the layout. She went over the pre-flight checklist with Captain Monroe. When everything checked out, she started the engines. Once those were online, she looked over the console again, looking for any abnormalities. When everything looked good, she requested permission to leave the hangar.

"Permission granted," came the reply.

She eased the controller forward and the ship started to move. She hit a button to get more thrust from it, and the ship moved forward as it lifted off. Once clear of the hangar, she looked at her instruments to make sure the way was clear before nudging the controller to get more speed from the craft. They flew out into space.

Captain Monroe gave her several maneuvers to perform, which she executed flawlessly. He only had to correct her once when she got a little too much speed out of the ship. He told her to ease back on the thrust. He then asked her to go through the procedures to jump to light speed. When Evalycer was ready, she made a brief jump to light speed, then brought the engines back to impulse.

When Evalycer had done all the skills asked of her, she flew back to the hangar and requested permission to land. She flew back in, turned the ship around, and landed with hardly a bump. She powered down the engines, went over the post-flight checklist, and blew out her breath quickly as she turned to Captain Monroe.

"I'm sure you're aware that if you don't pass the fighter portion of the test there is no need to continue with the cargo test," Captain Monroe said.

"Yes, sir," Evalycer said. Had she done something wrong? He never said anything out in space except for the one thing to correct. Maybe she'd done so badly that he couldn't say anything while out there.

"Let's head over to the cargo ship," he said with a grin.

"Awesome!" Evalycer said.

Lieutenant Langston snickered.

"He likes to scare people like that," she said.

They got into the cargo ship and again she started the pre-flight check, then started the engines.

Half an hour later, she flew back into the hangar. Once the engines powered down, Captain Monroe turned to Evalycer.

"Congratulations!" he said. "You are now a certified pilot."

"Yes!" Evalycer said as she smiled and pumped her fist in the air. She shook Captain Monroe's hand.

He turned to Lieutenant Langston, who pulled out a keepsake paper certificate and handed it to Captain Monroe, who signed his name and handed it to Evalycer.

"That's the one you can hang on your wall," he said. "We've sent the official one to your tablet as well as to Governor Atouu's office, and the Department of Space Travel. You are certified to fly any ship. Your license will need to be renewed every ten years."

Evalycer held that paper certificate carefully in her hands and smiled. She was a pilot! Her parents would be so proud of her.

She sped home to tell her parents the news and show them her certificate.

"I knew you'd do it," her father said, looking proudly at the certificate. "You're so smart, and you catch onto things very quickly."

"Let's go out to dinner to celebrate!" her mother suggested.

Evalycer looked at the time. She had a couple of hours before she had to be at the meeting.

"Sure!"

"Would you like to invite Erik?" her father asked.

"Yeah, I think I would!"

She contacted Erik, who happily said he'd meet them at the restaurant.

Evalycer and her parents arrived at the same time as Erik.

"Erik, these are my parents, Miranda and Jaiy," Evalycer said.

"Nice to finally meet you, Erik," said her father.

"Nice to meet you as well," he said.

Everyone enjoyed dinner, and Evalycer's parents seemed to like Erik. They asked him about his work, and he entertained them with his stories of his projects gone wrong. Evalycer hadn't heard some of the stories and they kept her mind off of the upcoming events in the faction.

After dinner, Evalycer drove with Erik to the meeting. He promised he'd take her straight home afterwards.

The meeting that evening had a different feel to it than usual. Everyone was more subdued and less talkative. Luckily Evalycer had become adept at hiding things in her mind since she had to hide her true feelings about everything in that group now.

Erik now told them how to set the explosives that would blow up the offices. He had done some studying himself over the weekend, learning all about explosives from the information Alexei gave him. Being technically inclined helped him understand all that this job entailed.

After the meeting, Erik drove Evalycer home.

"Do you want to come inside?" she asked as he walked her to her door.

"No, I've got to get home and start figuring stuff out for this," he told her.

He leaned down and kissed her lips gently.

"Can we go out tomorrow?" he asked.

"Sure," she agreed. "I'll get my homework...I don't have homework anymore! Ha! I'm going to take a ship out after work for a little while, then I'll come home to change and you can pick me up then."

"Okay, contact me when you're ready."

She put in the code for the door. It slid open, and she stepped inside, and with a smile to Erik, she let the door close again.

The next day, as Evalycer got ready for her date, she thought about all that was going on in the faction. It bothered her that everyone, especially Erik, was so eager to kill people. Outside of the meetings Erik was kind and caring. At the meetings, he made his thoughts very clear about wanting to take out the government, and she'd noticed the glint in his eye when he spoke about setting up the explosives.

During their date, Evalycer enjoyed herself, but was less talkative than usual. She had to be careful about what she thought about while out in public, knowing anyone could read her mind. She stuffed her feelings away, and tried to act like her usual sarcastic self.

On the drive home, Erik mentioned her mood.

"You don't seem yourself tonight," he said.

Evalycer sighed.

"I'm just concerned about this whole killing thing," she said. "How can you be so excited about it?"

"I'm not real excited about it, but Alexei said we didn't have much choice. We need change and Atouu won't listen to the people. He's immoral and it's horrible how everyone spies on everyone else. Two years ago, right after my dad was killed, Atouu had my mother hauled in for questioning and she ended up being detained overnight."

"Why?"

"While she was out shopping she was upset and dared to think that maybe my dad's death wasn't just a prisoner escape. Atouu had been trying to get my dad to work for him here, instead of commuting to Aknor. He knew my dad was good and wanted him for his security team, but my dad declined. It seemed to my mom that Atouu thought if he couldn't have him, no one could. Alexei has looked into this and hasn't found anything conclusive, but it all seems very suspicious."

"That's horrible," she said quietly.

"Plus who knows what else he does that's not in our best interests. If we don't get rid of him permanently, the group will be in danger when he figures out it was us who tried to take over the government."

Evalycer didn't like what she was hearing, especially coming from Erik, someone she loved and cared for. It made her more resolved to tell the governor what was going on.

Now that she had her pilot's license, Evalycer took a ship out every day after work. She took Erik with her one time. He nervously gripped the arm rests, his hands turning white as he did so, but once up in the air, he relaxed.

"You're really good at this," he told her.

"I've always wanted to fly out into the stars ever since I was a little girl," she told him. "I want to visit different systems and explore."

"As long as you come home for dinner," he joked.

"Is that a marriage proposal?" she said, looking sideways at Erik.

"Uh…um…" he stammered.

"I'm joking! We're too young, anyway," she decided.

Back on the ground, they went to their meeting. The meetings used to be one of the highlights of Evalycer's day. Now, she dreaded going. Her part in this now would be to set the explosives to take out the floor that Atouu's offices were on.

Another by-product of the meetings were that she ended up with a headache afterward. Not only because of trying to read minds, but because it made her ill to think of what they were doing.

She had enough information to do something about it. She knew the when, where, and how, but who to tell?

Evalycer became worried that the morning probe at work would turn up something. She still took the probe-blocker, but every time she went through, she held her breath. She tried manipulating the guards to skip her. She only tried that a couple of times. That was a crime in Atouu's eyes, so she had to find other ways to try to get around the probe. Hopefully she wouldn't have to do it for much longer.

With pilot school over, Evalycer had time to kill before the meetings on the days they met. Most of the time she took a ship up just to get away and admire the view of the systems. That was the only time she felt totally free of everything going on in her life at the moment. Sometimes she took Reina with her to get some quality girl-time together. With her busy schedule she'd missed hanging out with her friend, only seeing her at lunch most days.

When she went out on her own, Evalycer had thoughts of leaving for good, but she couldn't do that to her parents. They'd done all that they could to give her the life she had, making sure she could live her dreams. On the days of the meetings, she'd take the ship up, then go home and sit in her room meditating, trying to get into a better frame of mind.

No one suspected her of reading minds—yet. Evalycer hid her thoughts well, but if they ever tried to do a full and complete mind-probe on her, they'd find out about her betrayal.

At the next meeting, Alexei reminded the group that the takeover would be happening in one week. Evalycer's stomach turned when they started talking about her group's part in it.

Erik told Evalycer that although her part in this scheme had become bigger than he or she had wanted, he would still try to keep her away from it as much as he could.

"Your part is to help set up the explosives," he reiterated. "But that doesn't mean it's all on you. I can have you just take the items in and someone else can set them up."

"That would be helpful," she told him with a half-smile. "I don't even want to do that."

"I know, but I have to tell Alexei you're doing something. Other than that, you'll help clear the building of the workers there. I think you can handle that."

"That'd be preferred to killing people."

As the day got closer, Evalycer panicked, trying to think of how to stop this plot. She made up her mind that the only thing she could do was go to Atouu's office the next day and tell his assistant.

Evalycer started to wring her hands as she waited in line that morning, her eyes darting around nervously, looking at all the security personnel that stood at the entrance, checking everyone with the mind-probe. Part of it was because of what they'd find if she hadn't taken the probe-blocker, but also because of what she was about to do. What she had to do.

Once through the line, she went straight to the upper floor to Atouu's offices. An assistant sat at a desk in front of the long hallway where the offices branched off.

She took a deep breath, then let it out to try to relax.

"I need to speak to Governor Atouu, please," Evalycer said quietly.

"I'm sorry," the man said, looking up from his computer. "He doesn't speak with the interns. You'll have to send a memo with whatever it is you want to speak to him about. Maybe he'll get to it."

"He'll want to hear what I have to say," she said firmly.

"Everyone says that."

"It's life or death."

"Heard that before, too."

Evalycer sighed.

"Someone is going to try to kill Governor Atouu in two days."

The man's wide-eyed expression told Evalycer that she'd gotten his attention.

"I'll be right back," the man said.

"Yeah, I thought you might," she said.

He disappeared into one of the front offices.

Evalycer shifted nervously from foot to foot until the man brought out someone who Evalycer recognized as one of Atouu's assistants.

"Come with me, please," the assistant said.

Evalycer followed her into her office. The woman shut the door quickly and indicated Evalycer should sit in the chair in front of the desk.

"I am Olivia Marshall, second assistant to Governor Atouu," said the woman. "You say that someone is going to attempt to kill the governor in two days. How do you know this?"

Evalycer had to be careful about how she told her the information. She didn't want to incriminate herself, but didn't think there was much of a way around that. She tried part of the truth.

"I'm dating someone in this group that is trying to take over the government and put Atouu out of office," Evalycer explained. "At first it was just a takeover, but now it's moved into hostages and killing."

"And how did you find all this out?" Ms. Marshall asked skeptically.

"I read his mind."

"And we're just supposed to believe you? Who are you?"

"I'm Evalycer Nicholls. I work downstairs in the security department as a paid intern. I've been out in the field with Jax, and…"

"You're the girl who Ian speaks highly about."

Shit. My reputation precedes me.

"Yes," she said out loud.

"And when is this allegedly happening?"

"In two days, when Atouu is staying late to work on his next speech."

"They have his schedule?"

"Yes."

Ms. Marshall sat there, looking at Evalycer, but Evalycer knew she was thinking about how to proceed with this information. "We'll have to do a mind-probe on you, to make sure what you're telling us isn't just a fabrication. How was this never found in the morning probe?"

"I can hide my thoughts and block them from being probed."

"Such skill in someone so young," Ms. Marshall quipped.

"Do the mind-probe," Evalycer snapped. "It'll show you what's been going on."

Ms. Marshall made a couple of calls and took Evalycer down to Ian's private office. He and Jax both had a look of concern when she came in.

"What's this all about, Miss Nicholls?" Jax whispered.

"I have information about a plot to kill Governor Atouu," she told him.

Evalycer sat in the chair across from Ian. As it was procedure, Ian would first attempt to read Evalycer's mind.

Ian sat and stared at Evalycer, reading her mind. She knew he was good at reading minds, and could find things that were hidden. Wanting to see how well he could do that, and to show Ms. Marshall she could keep things hidden, she attempted to keep a few thoughts from Ian's probe.

After a few moments, Ian took a deep breath and blinked several times.

"What she said is true," he said. "But there were some blank spots that I had to peel away to get to, and some things that were still blank."

Evalycer smiled smugly at Ms. Marshall, whose wide-eyed expression conveyed her surprise that Evalycer had told the truth.

"We'll bring the probe unit in to get at those spots," Ian said.

By the time they located the mind-probe unit, Evalycer knew that the probe-blocker had worn off. Jax aimed the mind probe unit toward Evalycer's head. The probe brought all thoughts to the front of the person's mind, allowing the person using the probe to better read the thoughts of the person. The probe also recorded its findings. Evalycer knew that her involvement in this plot would come to the forefront, but her part had mostly been observing once the plans had changed.

After the mind-probe recorded what it read, Ian and Jax both turned to Ms. Marshall.

"We will need to keep this quiet," Ian said. "We'll take necessary precautions to keep Governor Atouu safe with this information. But this doesn't leave this office. We'll make sure the assistant at the door also doesn't say anything." He turned back to Evalycer. "I'm really disappointed in your involvement in this. You had a bright future in security here."

"I never wanted to work here. I only did it because I had to, and because the faction wanted information from here, though I wasn't able to get much of what they wanted."

She had been able to keep her part in getting Atouu's schedule buried in her mind. She had made sure that everything she had told Ian and Jax was easy to find, and she made her actions in the group a little less easy to find, but still available to the probe.

"What's going to happen to me?" Evalycer asked. "If they find out it was me, I'm dead."

"There is no way they'll know it was you," Ian explained. "You were here in my office to help with a case. You've been here before, so it won't look suspicious. In the meantime, your security clearance is revoked back to entry level. You can go back to your desk and we'll figure out what to do with you later."

Evalycer went back to her desk and tried to calm her still-shaking hands by opening and closing them rapidly. She turned on her computer and started on her work that she could do without the higher security clearance, her shaking hands hitting the wrong keys as she typed.

Later that afternoon, Jax called Evalycer into his office. Ian was there, too.

"We've decided that you will be able to finish out your internship for the rest of this year," Jax said. "You will have only minimal security clearance, and you will be going out into the field with me. You will submit to a mind probe by Ian every day until this faction is taken down. If you do not agree to these terms, you will be jailed along with the rest of the faction. Do you accept these terms?"

Jail? That word spun around in her head for a moment. She hadn't thought about the consequences of getting caught when she joined this group. But then they were only supposed to take over the government, not kill anyone.

"Yes, sir," she agreed.

"There may be more discipline later on, but for now, that's it. You can go," Ian said.

Evalycer got up and walked quickly out of the office and back to her desk.

She put her face in her hands and tried to steady her breathing, but she'd nearly been sent to jail.

Damn this faction! And how could I think we'd be successful in doing this in the first place? How could I be so stupid!

Chapter Eighteen—The Attack

Luckily, there was no meeting that night. Evalycer stayed home and in her room, curled up on her bed, trying to stave off the headache that recurred about that time every day.

Her mother knocked on her door. Evalycer beckoned her in.

"Dinner is ready," her mother said.

"I'm not hungry right now," Evalycer said.

"Are you okay? You've seemed kind of depressed lately."

"I might be coming down with something," she told her mother. "I've had a headache for a while and I've been queasy. I didn't even take a ship out to fly today after work."

"I'll make you some Ennek Root soup to settle your stomach," her mother said.

"Thanks."

Her mother closed the door, and Evalycer pulled the bed coverings over her head.

This wasn't how this was supposed to turn out, she thought. *I just wanted Atouu out of office. I'm not going to be responsible for killing him.*

At work the next day, security had been tightened. Evalycer had taken her probe-blocker, but it still made her nervous. In addition to the probe-blocker, everyone had to be physically checked before going inside. The women and men were separated into groups. When Evalycer's turn came, she had to spread her arms and legs out to be patted down. Security gave her the all-clear and she walked quickly to her floor and her desk.

"What's going on?" she asked Nita as she passed her desk.

"An anonymous communication came in yesterday," she whispered. "It said that everyone in the building was in danger, especially Governor Atouu. So far security hasn't turned up anything, but the message did say it wouldn't happen for a couple of days, but they're being cautious. I don't know what Atouu's security team is planning, and I couldn't tell you if I did. All I know is the threat is being taken seriously."

Evalycer went to her desk and turned on her computer. As it booted up, she sat and stared out the window.

They're calling it an anonymous tip. Her vision blurred for a moment indicating that she had a headache coming on again. With her computer up, she started working on the last part of the last module she had to complete. She knew that once she finished, she'd be put into the field permanently with Jax. While that strengthened her feelings that Atouu needed to be out of office, killing him wasn't the way to go. Hopefully another option could be found.

Because of her pounding headache, it took Evalycer until lunchtime to finish. Nita came over to her desk.

"Are you feeling okay?" she asked.

"I've had a headache for a week," she told her. "And my stomach hasn't felt great."

"Would you like to go home early?"

Evalycer thought about that. She didn't have any more work to do on the computer, but she didn't want to disappoint Jax.

"Jax wants me to go out in the field with him, and…"

"If he can't see that you're ill and can't work, he's got something wrong with him," Nita said firmly. "If you want to go, I'll talk to him."

"That would be great," Evalycer said, forcing a smile. She turned off her computer, gathered up her belongings, and left.

Evalycer arrived to an empty home. Her mother was still at the Academy and her father at his job. They would be home much later.

She went to her room, changed into more comfortable clothing, and sat on her bed and tried to read a book on her tablet to take her mind off of everything. When she read the same sentence three times over, she tossed her tablet across the room, hitting a pile of clothing on the floor.

"Fuck!" she exclaimed. She stood up and paced the floor. She couldn't concentrate on anything, and her head felt like it would explode. She stormed out of her room, out the front door, and went into the gym that she rarely used on the bottom floor of the building.

The equipment available was both virtual and physical. There was a Virtual Opponent program set up in the corner, but Evalycer didn't know how to use it, so she opted for the actual punching bag in another corner. She picked up the provided gloves and started to punch the bag, slowly at first, then developed a rhythm and punching faster. She worked up a sweat after just ten minutes of hitting that thing.

Twenty minutes later, she stopped and leaned on the bag to catch her breath. Sweat poured off of her as she gasped for air. Her anger and anxiety only slightly abated, she started kicking the bag as well as punching. Tears fell down her cheeks with each punch until she had no strength left. She sat down and sobbed. She pulled off the gloves and put her hands up to her face, resting her elbows on her knees. She felt her stomach churn and she barely had time to grab the trash can before she vomited into it.

What the hell is wrong with me? she thought. *I gotta get a grip!*

She wiped her mouth with a rag she found, then tossed that into the can as well. She wiped her eyes with her fists, took a deep breath, and got her emotions back under control.

Evalycer went back upstairs and showered, letting the hot water run over the back of her head. Her headache subsided after that.

She turned off the water and dried herself. As she dressed back in her room, she heard her mother in the living room, setting things down from work.

"Lees?" her mother called out.

Evalycer stuck her head out of her door.

"Yeah, I'm home," she replied. "I got let go early today because I wasn't feeling well."

"You've been working really hard lately. I'd hoped that once you got your license things would ease up a bit. Have they?"

"Mostly. There was a situation at work today and security was tight. I don't know what's going on, but I think it just was a bad day for me today."

"You may want to stay home for the rest of the week and take care of yourself."

The perfect reason to not participate in the Atouu plan.

"I think I will."

When Evalycer didn't show up for work the next day, Erik contacted her on her comm.

"Are you okay?" he asked.

"No, I'm not," she told him. "I was sent home from work yesterday because I'm ill. I vomited last night and my head feels like it's in a vice."

"So you won't be there tonight?"

"I doubt it. I can't get out of bed without my stomach turning. I'm sorry if it leaves you in a bind. I just can't do this tonight."

Erik sighed.

"I'll figure something out. Feel better. I'll try to come see you later."

Evalycer disengaged her comm and lay back in her bed. She didn't feel the least bit guilty for not being able to do her part in this thing tonight, but she wasn't into killing innocent people, including Atouu, even if she did hate his guts.

She contacted Reina. She needed someone to talk to, someone who knew what was about to happen, and just wanted to vent.

"I should have gotten out when you did," Evalycer said.

"I don't want to know what's going on," Reina said. "But I *do* want to know what's going on with you. Are you okay?"

"I'm just stressed out from all of this," Evalycer told her. "I'm more involved than I wanted to be."

Reina stayed on the line and spoke with Evalycer for half an hour.

"You're a good friend, Reina," Evalycer said as they said their goodbyes. "Thanks for letting me take up your lunch time."

"No problem," Reina told her. "I'll see you tomorrow."

I doubt that, Evalycer thought, but said aloud, "Take care," and disengaged the comm.

As they day went on, Evalycer didn't feel any better. The anxious feeling she'd had for the past week hadn't subsided even though she knew she wasn't going tonight. She couldn't stay in one place for long, and started to pace her room, which made her stomach queasy. Her arms felt fidgety. She shook them out, then rubbed them, trying to get that feeling out.

She knew the time that they were planning this explosion. As it got closer to the time, Evalycer lay on her bed again, curled up and covered herself with all of her bedding, leaving a hole through which to breathe. She heard her parents in the other room, coming home from their work day. Her mother knocked softly on the door. Evalycer didn't want to talk to anyone, and didn't answer. She heard her mother open the door to look in, checking on her. Evalycer pretended to be sleeping. She heard her mother shut the door again.

A few moments later, Evalycer heard a loud *boom!* across the city that rattled the windows of her building. Her eyes flew open, she drew in her breath quickly and held it for what felt like an eternity.

It's done.

Another explosion sounded. Tears flowed from her eyes and she sobbed into her bedding. She'd been a part of what just happened. She hoped her warning had been enough and everyone had gotten out. There'd be no way to know until later.

After crying uncontrollably for a few minutes after the last explosion, Evalycer wiped her eyes with her covers, and threw them off of herself. She grabbed a cloth from her side table and wiped her nose and eyes with it, then ran into the bathroom to throw up again.

It made her sick knowing what the faction had done, what *she'd* almost done. She heaved over the toilet until nothing else came out. She sat on the floor for a few minutes before she washed and dried her face, then went out to see the news.

"Evalycer! Oh my God," her mother said, hugging her daughter.

"What's wrong?" Evalycer asked.

"The government building was just blown up! Reports are coming in right now…"

They all turned to the holovision. The top of the building had collapsed, but most of the building was still standing. Only Atouu's offices were damaged, and two or three floors under it, where the security offices were, where Evalycer's office had been before her security was downgraded.

"I'm so glad you were ill today and stayed home," her father said. "You could have been in this mess."

More than you know, she thought.

They watched the reports for the rest of the evening. It finally came out that no one was in the building at the time.

"*The government received an anonymous tip two days ago, alerting the offices of the event. Atouu's office had taken every precaution to make sure the building was empty at the time of this attack…*"

Attack. That word stuck out at Evalycer. The attempt to take over the government, which started out as just a takeover, was now an attack.

The doorbell chimed. Miranda went to answer it.

"Lees, Erik's here to see you," she announced.

Evalycer, wrapped in a sweater, went to greet Erik. Her mother went back to watching the news.

"You really don't look well," he told her as she shut the door.

"No shit," she said quietly to avoid her parents hearing her.

"I thought you were just trying to get out of helping tonight," Erik admitted.

"Nope, I've been ill all day. I haven't been able to eat. The explosions woke me up."

"Is there some place we can go to talk?"

"We can talk in my room."

Evalycer led Erik to her room, turned on the lights, and shut the door. She sat on her bed and Erik took the chair across from it.

"How'd it go?" Evalycer asked.

"As you know by the reports, not well," Erik started. "They were tipped off and Atouu wasn't even there. Only a handful of people were still there when we set up the explosives. Dell and Jack didn't have much to do holding off people. Only security came up. One person was killed because Alexei had disengaged the Stun feature. Everyone kind of stayed away after that."

"Who was killed?" Evalycer hoped it wasn't Jax.

"I think it was one of Atouu's security guards."

Evalycer relaxed slightly.

"How did you all get out?" Evalycer asked.

"Once security stayed away and the explosives were set, we went out the fire exits to the outside stairs."

"Who was supposed to do reconnaissance? Didn't they know everyone was gone?"

"People went in this morning like they always do. We didn't have an exact count, and people started leaving throughout the day. We didn't know until after the fact that Atouu was moved to a secure location. If you weren't out sick today, we'd have

103

thought you were part of that. But then, you'd have told us the plan." He paused. "Wouldn't you?"

"If I'd been able to, sure," she lied. "But weren't you there today, too? Why didn't you know about this?"

"I got sent out into the field today, then left from there. I didn't know anything about an evacuation."

Evalycer stared out her window at the plumes of smoke still coming from the area of the government building.

"How can you be so calm about this? We were going to kill people."

"Atouu kills people! He invades their privacy! He needs to be gone, however we can get rid of him."

Evalycer didn't say anything.

How could Erik be so nonchalant about this whole thing?

"Well, I'm glad I was sick so I didn't have to do this."

"Maybe you were the one who tipped them off," Erik argued.

Evalycer worked hard to keep her face from registering the truth.

"You'd better take that back, Erik," she demanded.

Erik sighed heavily.

"I'm sorry," he said softly. "I don't want to fight."

"I don't either, seeing as I'm going to hurl again any minute."

Erik looked sharply at Evalycer, who shook her head. "I'm not actually going to vomit right now. But this whole fucking thing does make me sick."

Erik leaned over and ran his hand down Evalycer's face.

"I love you, Lees," he said.

She took his hand in hers.

"I love you, too. I'll be glad when everything about this is over. It's been stressful, to say the least."

Erik stood up, kissed the top of Evalycer's head, and left.

Evalycer turned on the holovision in her room to learn about any updates on the explosions. So far the authorities didn't have anyone in custody, but Evalycer knew that it was only a matter of time before the authorities got them or the faction came after her.

The sun's rays had a hard time penetrating the smoky air the following morning. All the government employees were told to not report to work that day which worked to Evalycer's advantage since she still felt sick to her stomach. She got out of bed and went to the kitchen to make a cup of Stimulating Tea to drink with the hopes that it would make her feel better. Her mother was there already, making breakfast for Jaiy and herself.

"Do you want anything, Lees?" her mother asked.

"No," she said. "I'm just going to make myself some tea."

"Sit down and I'll do it for you," her mother said.

Evalycer didn't argue, and sat down where she couldn't see the holovision or the smoke through the window. Her mother brought a mug of hot tea over a moment later.

"Still no news on who did this," her father stated.

"Hopefully it was a one-time thing and they catch the idiots who did it," her mother said.

Evalycer sputtered into her tea. She set the mug down and coughed to get the tea back where it should be going down her throat.

"Are you okay?" her father asked.

"Yeah," Evalycer said, clearing her throat. "Breathed in when I shouldn't have."

Her mother and father finished their breakfast and got their things together for work.

"Will you be okay today?" her mother asked, hand on the button to open the door.

"Yeah, I'll be fine. I'm starting to feel better already."

"I'll see you after work, then," her mother said, and she and Jaiy left for work.

Later in the day, the news revealed the Atouu had been taken to a secret safe house last night where he stayed through the night with his family and advisors. They would continue to work from there until the government building was repaired or they found another suitable location for the offices.

Evalycer got a message on her comm from Alexei. He wanted everyone to gather at a new meeting location that night. He wanted to go over what happened and wanted everyone to submit to a mind-probe.

I'm getting sick of these fucking mind-probes, she thought. She sent a message back, saying if she felt better she'd be there. A message came straight back.

"Be there or we'll come to you."

That settles that, then.

Evalycer left for the meeting before her parents returned home from work. She didn't want to explain to them why she was leaving while feeling ill. She felt somewhat better, but the headache came on again as she got closer to the new meeting place.

She sat in her vehicle for a few moments to get her mind ready. She didn't think that they'd have a mind-probe unit there, but wanted to be ready for it just in case. Evalycer thought about taking the probe-blocker, but if Alexei didn't see *anything*, he'd know she was hiding something. She'd have to trust her abilities.

Evalycer went inside the office and found the room they were meeting in. She waved to Erik across the room. He came over to her and kissed her cheek quickly.

"How are you feeling?" he asked.

"Like I'd rather be in bed," she said. "But Alexei threatened to come to my home, so I had to come."

Alexei stormed in at that moment.

"I want to find out who notified the government about our plans," he growled. "Everyone will wait here as we call people in one by one to read their minds. We'll start with the group leaders first."

Alexei called a name and the woman followed him into the next room. She came back a few minutes later.

"Erik, you're next," she announced.

"Be back in a few," he said, and he went into the next room.

He came back a few minutes later.

"Piece of cake," he said, sitting next to her again.

"What'd they do?" she asked.

"Just read my mind. He's very good at doing that without a mind-probe unit."

Evalycer felt relieved that there was no mind-probe unit.

There's no way he'll find out what I've done, she thought.

After all the group leaders had been called in, they started to call in everyone else. Evalycer was the fourth person to be called. She squeezed Erik's hand and walked confidently into the office.

"We're going to read your mind and see if you were the one to tip off the government," Alexei said, raising an eyebrow. "Unless there is anything you'd like to admit?"

"Nope, nothing," she replied.

Alexei looked into her eyes, reading her thoughts. Little did he know that she had become adept at hiding things while working with this faction. She left everything out about her illness and her talks with Erik, but had hidden everything else well.

"Sorry for the intrusion," he said, blinking his eyes. "We just had to be sure. You weren't there that night and it looked suspicious."

"I understand," she said, getting up to leave.

"Send in Lucas."

Evalycer went into the room and called out for Lucas to go in next.

"No problem, right?" Erik asked.

"Nope, no problem," she said. "I really need to get back home now. My head is pounding again."

"Have you seen the doctor for this?"

"No, not yet. If I'm not better by tomorrow, I'll go. See you later," she said.

Erik kissed her and she went to her vehicle. She felt as if she'd been holding her breath, and sat and breathed in deeply for a few minutes before heading home.

Her parents were already home when she returned.

"Where did you go?" her mother asked. "I thought you'd still be in bed."

"I needed to get out of the house. I feel like I've been cooped up for too long and needed some fresh air. I drove around with my windows open and felt a little better."

She hated lying to her parents, but she couldn't tell them where she'd actually been.

"If you're up to it, dinner is almost ready," her mother said.

"I think I do have an appetite again," Evalycer said.

Evalycer ate heartily at dinner with no ill effects afterward. She went to her room and started to feel much better. Her head stopped hurting and she felt like herself again.

All the stress is finally leaving my body, she thought. *I passed the mind-probe and Alexei has no reason to suspect me anymore. I can put this all behind me now.*

Evalycer got a message from Nita, telling her that they were all going back to work the next day and gave her the new address if she felt well enough to come back to work. She messaged Nita back.

I'll be there bright and early tomorrow.

When she awoke the next morning, Evalycer surveyed how she felt. No headache and her stomach wasn't flip-flopping. She got up and dressed, then went out to eat breakfast with her parents.

"Feeling better?" her father asked.

"Much better," she told him. "I'm going in to work today."

"Just take it easy and don't try to do too much," her mother said.

"Oh, I plan on only doing the bare minimum today."

Evalycer left at the same time as her parents, driving the opposite way. She got to the new building location and got in line with everyone else for the mind-probe, but when they got to her, security waved her through.

Confused, she went to find Jax.

"Why was I waved through today?" she asked.

"We've arranged for you to not have to go through the morning probe this week," Jax told her. "With everything that's been going on, we thought it prudent to have you skip it."

"Awesome," she said, and she started back to her office. Jax stopped her.

"You'll be working up here with me for a while," he told her. "While the threat to Atouu has passed, we want to keep an eye on you. We've already told Nita that you'll be up here. We told her that you'll be out in the field most of the time now, and won't be under her supervision anymore."

"She's not in trouble, is she?" Evalycer asked. She liked Nita, and hadn't thought of her own actions as having an effect on her.

"She's not in trouble," Jax assured her. "But we want to make sure you follow every rule from here on out. You will be doing field work so no need to be in Nita's office any longer."

"Okay," Evalycer replied.

Jax and Evalycer went out into the streets that day. This was the part of the government that they had been trying to overthrow—the reading of minds without permission. Jax had been ordered by Atouu to make Evalycer read minds. Jax couldn't force her to, though he did try to coerce her into doing it, but it wasn't in him to do that.

"I'll just tell Ian what he wants to hear," Jax said. "I understand your hesitance. I was like you once, but I eventually bent to the rules. I'm sorry I can't do more for you."

"It's okay," Evalycer told him. "I figure I'll be out of security here at the end of this year anyway. Where do you think they'll move me?"

"Probably some place like Interrogation. You're good at reading minds, so they can put you there to draw out the thoughts of criminals instead of putting you out here to read minds."

At the end of the day, they got back to the offices and filled out a report. Ian believed Jax when he told him Evalycer had done a great job in reading minds that day.

"I knew she'd come around," he said, looking at Evalycer.

She gave him a sarcastic smile, then turned and left to go home.

Later that week, Ian called Evalycer into his office again.

"Atouu wants the names of the people responsible for the attack," Ian said.

"I can't do that," she said, taken aback. "If I do that, they'll come after me and probably my family."

"We need to know who did this and arrest them. You have to tell us who it is."

"I can't!"

Ian sighed.

"We'll put you and your parents in protective custody in another system with military presence. You'll be safe."

"You can do that?"

"Yes. I'll arrange for your parents to get transferred there."

"My mother works at the Academy and my father works security for a business. Can you guarantee that my parents will get the same jobs?" Evalycer asked.

"Absolutely," Ian assured her.

Evalycer mulled that over. Her parents knew nothing about her involvement in this government takeover. She'd have to tell them everything, and didn't know how her parents would respond to that. Their smart daughter getting involved with a group like that? Disappointment, for sure.

"Okay," she said hesitantly. "But you make the arrangements first and they are sent there, then I'll tell you who it is."

Ian picked up his comm and contacted some people to make the arrangements. After half an hour of talking with people, it was all set. This was another part of Atouu's government—making people disappear. At least this time, it worked to Evalycer's advantage.

"I'll need to tell my parents what's going on," Evalycer said.

"Go home and talk to them," Ian said. "They will be told tomorrow that they are being transferred to Darantha."

Evalycer arrived at home before her parents. She wanted to have some time to collect her thoughts and prepare for their disappointment. It wouldn't be the first time she'd disappointed them, but this time would be the biggest.

She heard her mother come home and head into the kitchen to start dinner. Her father came home a few minutes later. Evalycer took a deep breath.

Time to do this, she thought, and she went out to talk with them.

"How are you feeling today?" her mother asked.

"Better," she said.

"I was worried about you, you know. Glad you're feeling better."

"I have something to talk to you and Dad about," Evalycer said, voice shaking.

"What's up?" her father asked.

Half an hour later, her parents sat in stunned silence. Evalycer could barely breathe, waiting for her parents to blow up, shout, something. The look of disappointment on their faces was nearly unbearable.

"We knew something was wrong," her father finally said softly. "It wasn't like you to be so withdrawn, even while ill."

Evalycer nodded, but said nothing.

"While we recognize that you were trying to do something good, this was not the way to do it," her mother said.

"I realize that now," Evalycer said.

"We have to leave our home again," her father said sternly. "I have to find a job again…"

"No, you don't," Evalycer said. "I told them I wasn't giving them any information unless they guaranteed you'd both have jobs wherever they sent us. You will get your transfer orders tomorrow."

"What will you do?" her mother asked.

"I'll find something. I have my pilot's license now, so I can get a job flying cargo ships or join the Interrogation unit. I'd be in high demand with my mind-reading ability."

"We're so disappointed in your involvement, Evalycer," her father said.

"I know," she said, wiping her eyes. "I'm so sorry I got involved and put you in jeopardy. It wasn't my intention to put anybody at risk. When I found out what the group was going to do, when they changed their plan, I had to do something. I wasn't into killing anyone."

Her parents rose from their seats.

"We'll start packing up tonight. I'm sure this will have to happen quickly," her mother said.

"The sooner the better for everyone," Evalycer said. "I'm not telling them anything until you're far away from here, then I'll join you."

After dinner, they spent the rest of the evening packing up their life there on Startia.

Jaiy and Miranda got the transfer information the next day, effective as soon as they could get there. They finished the rest of the packing that night, and Jaiy hired a moving company to pick up their belongings to take to Darantha the next day.

"I'll be there as soon as I can," Evalycer told her parents.

Evalycer would stay at their home for a few more days, until her parents were safely in their home on Darantha. Since all of her belongings had been packed and moved, she slept on her bed in a sleeping bag, and had kept a few changes of clothing that could be easily taken with her in her bag.

At work, she and Jax went out into the streets as usual, looking for those who had intent to break the law. She knew that she'd done the right thing by telling Atouu about the plan, but still disagreed with his politics. Luckily she'd be leaving soon and

114

wouldn't have to do this kind of work for a corrupt government ever again.

Her father contacted her to let her know that they were in their home. The new home had security that came with it as well as a military presence in the area since they were near the Royal Planet Fleet's base.

With that news, Evalycer went in to talk with Ian.

"Okay, I can give you that info you wanted," she said.

She only gave the names of the people in charge, namely Alexei and his subordinates. She left Erik and Theo out of it, although she knew that both Erik and Theo had bigger roles in the faction then she wanted to admit. But she wanted to protect Erik, even though she knew they were over. Once he figured out it was her who gave the government the names, he'd want nothing to do with her.

"We'll make the arrests tonight," Ian said. "Want to come with us?"

"Hell no!" she said. "I don't want my name or face anywhere near this."

"Good luck to you," Ian said. "You had a promising future here."

"My politics don't mesh with Atouu's. I think it's wrong to read people's minds without their permission just to make sure people stay in line."

Ian contacted Jax and a few more officers to go make the arrests. Evalycer, finally finished with her internship there, drove the opposite direction, back home, or what was left of her home. She'd hop on a flight out to Darantha that evening, leaving this place behind her.

At her home, she packed up everything she had into her bag and looked around. She'd miss the good times she'd had there on Startia, but wouldn't miss the drama.

The door chime interrupted her thoughts. She put her bag down and went to answer the door.

115

"Hi, Erik," she greeted.

"Going somewhere?" he asked, noticing her bag on the floor of the empty room.

"My parents got transferred to another system," she said. "I had a few things to finish up before leaving."

"Yeah, I'll say you did."

"What do you mean?"

"It was you, wasn't it?"

"What are you talking about?"

"It was you who tipped off the government about our plan to kill Atouu."

Evalycer didn't back down from the accusation.

"Yes, it was," she told him.

Erik paced the room.

"Why would you do that? We planned this whole thing to overthrow his government, to make things better, and you fucking ruined it!" he whined.

"I told you I wasn't into killing anyone, no matter who it was. Innocent people would have been killed."

"You know how long we planned this, and I made sure you were kept out of the killing part. All you had to do was take the explosives to the office."

"And I would've still been part of killing those people! Innocent people, not just Atouu. And he didn't deserve to be killed. I just wanted him out of office."

"You'll have a price on your head so big that if you ever come back here, you'll be killed."

"No one but you will know."

"I'm going to tell them."

It shocked Evalycer that Erik would tell them, after the time they'd spent together, being in love.

"I thought you loved me, Erik. I guess this is what love means to you?"

"This is bigger than us, Evalycer. This is about taking down a corrupt government, and *you* blew it. They've arrested Theo, and they're looking for Alexei, but they can't find him."

"I tried to keep Theo and you out of my info to them. Guess they found out about him, anyway." Evalycer picked up her bag to leave. "I hope they don't find you," she said sincerely.

Erik softened his stance, but only for a moment. He pushed back his shoulders and said, "I hope you're good at looking over your shoulder and hiding."

"I'm leaving here, so no need to worry. Too many bad memories," she said.

"Even with us?"

"Well, I apparently didn't mean that much to you if you're going to turn me in. Do it, but I'll be long gone by the time they come looking for me."

She pushed past Erik, who tried to grab her arm to stop her. She shrugged it off.

"Don't touch me again!" she told him, eyes blazing.

She ran out to her vehicle, threw in her bag and got in. She gunned the engine and that was the last she saw of Erik, who had run out into the street, watching her drive away.

Evalycer arrived at the public transport station only a few minutes later, but as she drove around, she noticed several men watching her. She recognized one of the men as Alexei's security guard.

"Shit," she said and she drove past. The men ran after her, then ran to their vehicles, but she managed to ditch them in the crowded parking area.

Where can I go? she thought. *I can't take public transport now.*

The only other place she knew she could get a flight out was the pilot school. She turned her vehicle toward the school, hoping Alexei's men hadn't thought of going there, too.

Evalycer drove into the parking lot of the school and looked around. Seeing no one suspicious, she walked quickly into the hangar. She saw Mr. Kemp in the offices there. She tried to look casual as she walked into the office.

"Hi!" she greeted.

"There's my best student," Mr. Kemp said. "Taking another flight out today?"

"Absolutely," she said. "I might be gone most of the day. I just want to see the stars."

"No problem," said the hangar officer. "Just sign it out like always and we'll see you back this evening?"

"Sure," Evalycer said, but knowing she'd never come back.

She signed out the small ship she always used, then went to grab her bag from her vehicle. As she did so, she thought she saw Alexei's men driving in. She hurried back to the hangar with her bag.

"I just wanted to say thanks for everything you've taught me," she said to Mr. Kemp.

"It's been my pleasure," he said. "Have fun today."

Evalycer smiled, then walked over to the ship. She ran through the pre-flight sequence, then started the engines. She saw Alexei's men run into the hangar just as she punched the button to take off. She breathed with relief once she cleared the hangar.

"See ya, assholes," she said as she flew away from Startia, planning to never return to it again.

Not knowing to what extent Alexei's men would go through to get to her, she didn't fly straight to Darantha. She flew instead to Foridian, the nearest planet to Startia.

She had never gone through the asteroid belt before, and she remembered her father telling her about it many years ago. As she approached it she received a signal from the security outpost there.

"We'll escort you through the belt," they said.

They pulled her in with a tractor beam and put a shield around both their crafts to protect them from the asteroids. The security ship maneuvered around the asteroids carefully, avoiding the bigger asteroids. Some of the smaller ones hit the shields around the ships, bouncing off them. Once through, they bid her goodbye and she was off to Foridian. As she approached their space Evalycer asked for and received clearance to land at the public transport station.

She got out and went to talk with the hangar chief.

"Is there any possible way that someone can fly my ship back to Startia for me?" she asked. "I borrowed it but don't intend on going back anytime soon."

"Sure," the chief said. "I think I have someone going there tomorrow who can take it."

"And then do you have a ship I can rent to go to Aknor?"

"Are you in some kind of trouble?" the chief asked hesitantly.

"No, but I'm trying to ditch some guy who won't take 'No' for an answer. I'd rather not have him trace the ship to where I'm trying to go."

119

That was only slightly a lie. She didn't want Alexei tracking her wherever she ended up. Whether he took no for an answer was up in the air.

"Oh, gotcha," said the chief. "Yeah, I have a ship you can rent. Two hundred credits."

Evalycer pulled out her tablet to check her credit account. She had enough. Barely. She'd have just enough left over to get a cheap place to live until she got a job.

"Okay," Evalycer said.

He took her to a ship that he had available and asked to see her pilot license. She proudly pulled it up on her tablet for him to verify it and record the number. She paid the chief and she went on her way, but not to Aknor. She told the chief that in case anyone came looking for her. She instead turned toward Monta Nesta.

Her comm beeped. Evalycer pulled it off her belt and looked at it. It was Erik. She sighed and hit the button.

"What do you want?" she snapped.

"Where are you?" Erik asked. "Everyone's looking for you."

"Yeah, I know. Alexei's goons were at the transport station waiting for me. I had to change my plans."

"You need to come home," Erik said sternly. "We can work this out."

"The hell we can. You were going to turn me over to Alexei, and by the looks of it, you did that. I loved you, Erik, and this is how you show me your love?"

"They'll find you, Evalycer. They know you went to your pilot school and borrowed a ship. They'll find out from your instructor where you went."

"Well, I didn't tell him where I was going, and I've taken another ship," she said. "So they won't find me."

"They'll just follow the beacon that's on the ship. They'll find you."

Shit. I forgot about that.

120

She set her comm down and turned on the auto-pilot. She pulled up a schematic of the ship and located the beacon. She pulled a cover off the floor, found the correct wires and cut them.

"That won't be a problem anymore," Evalycer said, brushing her hands together.

"What do you mean?"

"No more beacon on the ship I'm on."

With that, she turned off her comm.

Evalycer did a lot of thinking on her trip to Monta Nesta. She'd contact her parents and let them know what's going on, then find a place to stay until things cooled off with Alexei and Erik. She hoped that they wouldn't figure out where she'd gone.

She arrived at Monta Nesta a few hours later. She pulled up the planet information on the ship's computer to find a suitable place to land. She wanted to stay away from the big cities, thinking that's where Alexei would start looking for her first. She picked a city as far away from the capital as possible and asked for and received permission to land at the public spaceport.

She grabbed her bag and disembarked her ship and looked around. It looked like any other spaceport—lots of ships of varying sizes, lots of people milling around. She needed to find the office to get the rental ship marked as "returned". She asked someone where to find it and they pointed her in the right direction.

Having taken care of the return of the ship, Evalycer needed to find a quiet spot to contact her parents. She walked to the park next to the spaceport. She located a bench in a semi-secluded area and sat down. She hit the code for her mother, who answered on the second buzz.

"Where are you?" her mother asked. "We've been so worried about you."

"I can't get to Darantha right now," Evalycer said. "Alexei's men were waiting at the transport station, so I couldn't leave from there. I borrowed a ship from the pilot school and flew to another planet—I'm not telling you which one in case they somehow find you. I'm no longer on that planet. I flew to another one in another ship. They will be looking for me for some time. I can't come home," she finished, voice shaking, wiping the tears that ran down her cheeks.

"We're safe, Evalycer, we have a safe building with military all around us. Can't you come here?"

"I don't want to chance it. I'll come when I think it's safe. I'll call you every day. Think of it as I've gone off to school. I'll be home before you know it."

"Do you need money?"

Evalycer didn't want to burden her parents with keeping her afloat financially, but she would need some money until she found a job.

"Maybe just a little. I have enough to get a place to stay until I find a job, but I won't have anything for food."

"We'll transfer some credits to your account and you can pay us back whenever." That meant she didn't want Evalycer to pay her back.

"Thanks, Mom."

"Here's your father," her mother said, and Evalycer heard her father's voice a moment later.

Evalycer assured her father that she'd be safe. She told him her plan and he agreed that it was best for now.

"We love you, Lees," he said.

"I love you too, Dad," she said, and she disconnected.

I really screwed up my life, she thought. *Not going to dwell on that now. I need a place to stay.*

The city—she wasn't sure of the name—looked like one big marketplace. Most of the low buildings had awnings on the front, advertising what they sold. Brightly painted stores lined the streets, luring people inside. Different vehicles sped past on the street as she passed people on the sidewalk, which made her nervous. She kept looking behind her, just to make sure no one followed her.

Evalycer walked slowly down the long street, looking into each store's windows. Near the end of the street she came up on a store that advertised custom weapons. She realized that if she was going to live on her own in a strange city, she'd better get some protection. She went inside.

"Hello," greeted the man sitting behind the counter. "Looking for something in particular?"

"Just looking for something to protect myself with," Evalycer said.

"Premade or custom?"

"I'm not sure, let me look around."

"Take your time," the man said.

Evalycer looked inside all the cases. She knew she wouldn't be able to buy a blaster since she wasn't authorized to have one, but a knife would do. There were some knives that she liked, but were too cumbersome for her to use effectively. She saw a knife in a shape she liked, but wanted something smaller, easier to carry with her.

"Can you make me something like this, but smaller?" she asked, pointing to the knife in the case.

The man came over and looked at it.

"Sure! How big do you want it?" he asked.

She thought about it for a moment, then told him the dimensions.

"I can have it ready by the end of the week," he said. "Fifty credits."

Evalycer pulled out her tablet to see if her parents had sent her the money. They had, much more than she expected.

"Okay, no problem," she said, and she made the purchase. "Do you happen to know if any place needs any help?" she asked.

"Actually, I can use some help two or three days a week. What experience do you have?"

She told him that she had a pilot's license, and that she had some experience handling some weapons.

"I'm a quick learner. I was the top of my class at pilot school, testing out before anyone else."

"Pilot's license? I could use someone to deliver orders to other planets in the system. It doesn't happen often, but it does happen. I have to close the shop when I do it. It'd be great to have someone else do it."

"Do I have the job?" she asked.

"Sure," the man said, shaking her hand.

He introduced himself as Lou. She didn't want to give her full name, in case anyone came looking for her.

"I'm Lees," she said. "Lees Miranda," using her mother's name for her last name.

"You can start tomorrow."

"I'll be here bright and early," she said with a smile.

Next order of business—find a place to live.

She walked into what looked like a decent neighborhood with clean streets and fairly new-looking buildings. She doubted she could afford to live there, though, but decided it wouldn't hurt to check since it was close to work.

Evalycer saw a rental sign outside of one building. She went to talk to the landlord, and the space was barely big enough for a bed and a chair. The tiny kitchen had a small refrigerator and a stove, but no oven. She could live with that.

"I'll take it," she told the man. "Can I move in right away?"

"Sure, if you'll clean it up, I'll knock off half the rent for the month."

"Deal!"

He gave her the code for the place, and she started cleaning right away. The landlord came back up later to inspect it, and was happy with it. She paid the half-rent for the month, and settled in.

By week's end, Evalycer had her knife. Lou brought it out to her as she sat at the counter, watching the store for him.

"It's a thing of beauty, I think," he said, unwrapping it for her.

The knife, twenty centimeters long, had a curved blade attached to a handle in the middle.

"That's beautiful!" Evalycer exclaimed.

"Thank you," Lou said. "It should work out nicely for your needs."

Lou gave her a sheath to keep it in. She attached it to her belt on the right side where she could easily and quickly grab the knife if she needed it. She hoped she'd never need it, but if Alexei or any of his men found her, she knew she'd have to use it. Hopefully she wouldn't have to use it on Erik, for as much as she hated Erik at that moment, she had loved him once, and didn't want any harm to come to him, at her hand or anyone else's. She would defend herself, though, no matter who Alexei sent to get her.

At home, she practiced taking the knife from her belt, unsnapping the closure and snatching the knife until she could do it in one fluid motion. She wanted to be prepared in case she needed to use it.

Evalycer made her daily call to her parents before she went to work.

"I may be able to come home soon," Evalycer told her parents.

Nothing had happened in the nearly six months that Evalycer had been on Monta Nesta. She'd been careful not to use her real name anywhere, and had stayed out of trouble.

"That's wonderful," her mother said. "Nothing has happened here at all. No one's come looking for you and no one's bothered us. I think you'll be safe here."

"I'll let Lou know that I'll be leaving and I can be there in a week," Evalycer said.

"We'll make sure your room is ready. Oh! Your rover finally got to us yesterday after we spoke."

"Great! Thanks, Mom," she said, and she disengaged the comm.

Evalycer got ready for work. She dressed and brushed her hair, pulling it back into a ponytail. After making sure her knife was attached to her belt, she drank her Elixir and started her walk to the shop.

Midway through the day, as Evalycer worked on a shipment in the back, she heard someone come into the shop. Lou was out front, so she kept working on arranging the boxes in the storage room.

Loud voices coming from the front made her stop working to listen to what was going on.

"I don't know anyone named Evalycer!" Lou shouted. "I don't know how many times I have to tell you."

Evalycer's heart felt like it would pound out of her chest.

Shit! They've found me.

Evalycer set down the box she'd been holding. She had two choices. She could run and leave poor Lou to defend himself against whoever was out there, or she could make her presence known and save Lou. It wasn't in her nature to be a coward, so after making sure her knife was securely on her belt, she went to the front.

"They're looking for me, Lou," she said firmly.

"Well, well," Theo said. "Looks like you were lying to us, old man."

"He wasn't lying to you," Evalycer said. "I never gave him my real name, to protect him."

"Aren't you the noble one," Theo said. "Maybe we'll let him live if you come with us right now."

"You let him leave now, or I don't come at all," she countered. She turned to Lou. "I'm sorry I've put you in this situation. I didn't think they'd find me. It took them a long time, though," she finished, looking at Theo and his men. "Not so great at searching for people, are you?"

"I see you haven't lost your sarcastic mouth. Okay, old man, you can go," Theo said, motioning for Lou to go out the back way.

Lou turned to leave, pausing as he passed Evalycer.

"Good luck," he whispered.

"You, too. I'm sorry about this."

A moment later she heard the back door slam, indicating Lou was safely out of the way.

"I thought we were friends, Theo," Evalycer said, trying to stall while she thought of something to get herself out of this situation.

"We were, until you turned us all over to the police," he said bitterly.

"How's Alexei? Still avoiding capture?"

"For the time being. He's gone underground. I, on the other hand, just finished serving four months in prison for conspiracy. I got out early after manipulating the minds of the board of directors to release me."

"Figures," she said. "You were always good at that."

"Enough chit-chat. Let's get going here. I'll take the knife off you, if you please," he said.

Evalycer took the knife out of its sheath and held it out to Theo. As he went to grab it, Evalycer sliced his hand with it, nearly severing two of his fingers. He screamed in pain, using his other hand to try to staunch the bleeding. The two other men came at Evalycer. She swung her arm around and the knife connected with one man's side. She pulled the knife and made a cut under his ribs. As he went down in pain, the other man grabbed Evalycer's ponytail and pulled her off balance. She stumbled, trying to get her feet under her again, but the man grabbed her in a bear hold, pinning both her arms so she couldn't use her knife effectively. She stabbed the knife into his thigh. He cried out in pain, but didn't let go. She twisted the knife in his leg, and he finally let go of her.

Breathing heavily, she turned around and saw that the men were incapacitated for the moment. She wiped the blood off her knife and put it back on her belt.

"Anyone follows me, and I'll do more than just injure you," she said coldly.

With that, she walked through the shop and out the back.

She saw Lou up the alley, sitting on some boxes.

"Are you okay?" she asked softly, touching his shoulder gently.

"Shaken, but okay," he said. He noticed the blood on her shirt. "Are you okay?"

She looked down at her shirt. "It's not mine," she said. "My knife performed well, though I didn't think I'd ever have to use it." She sighed. "Listen, I have to leave right now instead of the end of the week. I fear more people will come looking for me, even though I just threatened to kill anyone else who comes looking for me. I'm sorry for this."

"You've been a good employee, Lees," Lou said. "I wish you well."

They shook hands, and Evalycer walked quickly back to her apartment. She gathered up her things and put whatever would fit into a couple of bags she had, making sure she had a few cans of Elixir with her, just in case.

Evalycer spoke to her landlord on the way out.

"I'm sorry I have to leave right away," Evalycer said. "Family emergency that can't wait. I'm paid up to the end of the month, so hopefully you can find someone else to rent the place after that."

"I hope everything works out for you and your family," the landlord said.

"Thanks."

With that, Evalycer headed to the station to get a transport off Monta Nesta.

At the station, she found a transport heading to her home planet of Ennek. It was a risk, but she was running out of options. She wouldn't stay long, though. She had friends who would help her while she was there, then she'd head to Darantha.

The transport arrived on Ennek five standard hours later. As she walked out of the transport station, Evalycer noticed that not much had changed since she'd moved from there six standard years earlier.

Her daily calls to her friend Taniya had devolved to once a week. They were both busy in their careers, but they still made time for one another during the week.

Evalycer contacted her friend now.

"Hey, Lees," Taniya said. "You're calling earlier than usual. Things okay?"

"Things are better than okay," Evalycer said. "I'm back on Ennek!"

"Really? I'm so happy!"

They made plans to meet in a couple of hours. Evalycer used that time to contact her parents.

"I won't be there just yet, but soon," she told her father.

"What happened?"

"Alexei's men found me," she said, but left out all the details. "I'm on Ennek right now, and I'll be on Darantha in a couple of days. I don't think they'll come looking for me again."

"I hope not," her father said. "We'll see you in a few days, then."

Later that day, Evalycer met up with Taniya for dinner. She spotted Taniya at a table and waved. Taniya smiled broadly and ran up to hug her friend.

"I'm so glad you're back!" Taniya squealed.

"Me, too," Evalycer said. "Unfortunately it's only for a couple days."

"Why? What's going on?"

"I'll tell you as we eat," Evalycer said.

They sat down and ordered their food. Evalycer told her friend everything that had been going on.

"I'm on my way to Darantha to move back in with my parents," Evalycer concluded.

"You're not staying?" Taniya asked.

"No, I think my parents are afraid of me being on my own with all this going on. Besides, Darantha has a military presence, so they feel safer there and think I will, too. That brings me to my next question: can I stay with you for a couple of nights? Just until I leave?"

Taniya didn't hesitate. "Of course! It will be like old times, having a sleepover," she said.

After dinner, Evalycer got into Taniya's land-rover and her friend drove them to her home. Once inside, Taniya told Evalycer to make herself at home.

In the morning, Taniya had to leave for work. She gave Evalycer the code to the door so she could go out and reminisce in the city.

Evalycer did just that, roamed around the streets, visiting places she hadn't seen in years. It was too bad they'd had to leave, and even worse that she couldn't stay now. She didn't think anyone would come looking for her, but she couldn't be sure. Her threat might not have been enough deterrent for the faction.

All too soon, the time came for Evalycer to leave the following day. She and Taniya promised each other to keep in touch like they had been.

"I'll be closer, so maybe we can get together often," Evalycer said.

With that, they hugged and Evalycer went to the transport station to fly to Darantha.

Chapter Twenty-Three—Darantha

Nighttime had fallen by the time Evalycer arrived on Darantha. She contacted her parents and her father came for her a few minutes later.

"I'm so happy you're finally home!" he exclaimed, hugging his daughter.

"Me, too," she said.

At home, her mother was equally happy to see her daughter again.

"Your hair has gotten so long," her mother stated.

"Yeah, I didn't see any reason to have to cut it," she said. "I like it long."

Miranda showed Evalycer to her room. Her mother had set up for her just as it had been on Startia.

"Thanks for doing that for me," Evalycer said.

"We knew you'd be here, eventually," her mother said.

Her parents told her about the security system there in their building. No one could get past the system, as it was tied into the military's security.

"Living so close to the base has its advantages," Jaiy said.

"Speaking of the military," Evalycer said. "I was thinking about joining the Royal Planet Fleet."

"You are?" her parents asked in unison.

"Yes. What better protection than to join? I'm a good mind-reader, so hopefully I can join the interrogation unit there. And I'm a good pilot, too. They can put me anywhere and I'd be useful to them."

"If you're sure about this, we're behind you," her father said.

Her mother didn't say anything.

"Are you okay, Mom?" Evalycer asked quietly.

"We just got you back and you want to leave again," she said.

"I won't be far, and I can come visit on the weekends. But it won't be for a couple of weeks. I need to sign up first."

Evalycer waited a few days to let her decision sink in with her mother. She knew her mother was scared that she'd be called into a war, but Evalycer was already fighting her own war with the faction. She'd made a horrendous mistake in joining that faction, so now she tried to make it right again.

"I think you're doing the right thing," her mother said one night during dinner. "You're right. They wouldn't be able to get to you if you've joined the RPF."

"So you're okay with my decision?" Evalycer asked.

"You have my blessing."

"Thanks, Mom," she said with a smile.

First thing Evalycer did the next day was go to the recruitment center to sign up. The recruitment officer went over everything that she would have to do and what the expected outcome would be.

"It's a four year commitment," the officer told her. "You'll go to the training center to learn how to use weapons and learn to follow orders."

That would be the one thing that may trip her up— following orders. But she made up her mind that she would and could do it.

When everything was in order, Evalycer signed her name on the tablet. The officer stood up and shook her hand.

"Welcome, Cadet Nicholls," he said.

Evalycer went home to pack up a few things for her training camp, which started the next day.

"They don't waste any time, do they," her mother said.

"Today was the last day to register for the next session," Evalycer said. "Otherwise I would have had to wait another month."

Evalycer was sworn in the next day, which took place at the training center a few kilometers away from their home. Her parents came to watch the ceremony.

Evalycer proudly repeated the words of the oath and smiled at her parents as the ceremony ended.

"We're so proud of you, Evalycer," Miranda said, kissing her daughter's cheek.

~~~~~~~~~

After graduation ten weeks later, in which she graduated with top honors in Interrogating and piloting, they assigned Evalycer, along with a few others, to the base in Aldra, the capital of Darantha. What Mr. Kemp had said back on Startia was true, and Evalycer entered the RPF as a sergeant because of her pilot training.

She dressed in her purple and black uniform, and pulled her hair back into a long braid. Once she arrived at the base and joined her group, an officer led the group to the Interrogation and Security offices, where they met with several other members of the fleet, including Princess Maryllia Vance of Darantha, a Sergeant and Interrogator on base.

Evalycer was assigned to the same department as Sergeant Vance, who was second in command in the department.

"I just want to get a few things out right now," Sergeant Vance started. "While in this uniform, I am not a princess. Therefore, do not bow to me when you greet me. Please address me as you would any other fleet member here."

Evalycer smirked. She wasn't about to bow down to anyone, anyway.

After Sergeant Vance finished her introduction, they got on with their work.

Evalycer's work ethic impressed some of the higher-ups in the department. She liked the work and the atmosphere of the base, and she liked who she worked with.

It's so much different than working for Atouu, she thought.

As her time in the military went on, she became a valuable asset to the department, being promoted to Lieutenant after only a few months.

Evalycer heard from Taniya on Ennek that a few people had come looking for her there. Once Taniya told them she'd gone to Darantha, they left without any issues, though they vowed to find a way to get her.

During her first year as part of the RPF, Evalycer lived at home. Once she had a few job promotions under her belt, she could afford to buy her own home. She wanted something away from the noise of the city, and found something on the edge of Aldra, in a neighborhood of houses with gardens, and small shops within walking distance of her home.

Evalycer hoped that her being an officer would be enough to keep the threat of revenge for her betrayal away from her. Besides, she now could legally carry a blaster, and was a pretty good shot with it.

Thank you so much for reading Evalycer's War. If you enjoyed it, please consider leaving a review on Amazon or Goodreads and tell your friends about it! If you found any typos, please email me at jedi_anegram@hotmail.com.

I didn't know when I wrote The Elixir Deception that I'd like the character of Evalycer Nicholls so much. This book came about because Evalycer's story needed to be told. She will turn up again in Book Three of The Elixir Series. Who knows what she'll be doing next!

I'd like to thank the writing communities I'm a part of, both online and in Colorado. Aspiring Authors, Ink Authors, Sparkly Badgers of Facebook, SciFi Roundtable have all given me a wealth of knowledge and help anytime I ask. Pikes Peak Writers has been a great help with their yearly conference and monthly Write Brains. I love to learn and will probably never learn all there is about this writing stuff, but I'll have fun trying!

You can find my website at
https://jedianegram.wixsite.com/margenaadamsholmes

Feel free to Like my Facebook page
www.facebook.com/AuthorMargenaAdamsHolmes

Other books by Margena Adams Holmes

On The Line
Dark Harmony
The Elixir War
The Elixir Deception
Dear Moviegoer: Tales From Behind The Velvet Curtains

www.ingramcontent.com/pod-product-compliance
Lightning Source LLC
Chambersburg PA
CBHW020248150626
46552CB00020B/716